S0-BOD-327

"Are you going to come back?"

Rafe seemed to await her answer as intently as his daughter, their dual gazes penetrating clear to her soul. Almost as if he wanted her to come back as much as Sunny wanted her to…

And for a moment Mariah's desire to return had nothing to do with saving her job.

A whirl of emotion swept her, as unexpected as yesterday's tornado. How had this happened so fast? How had she not seen this coming?

Sunny had her grandma, but that didn't mean the child wouldn't start to love her, only to be hurt when the time came for her to leave. As for Rafe—even if he did have feelings for her beyond the basic, which she doubted, he was the last kind of man she needed to fall for. There was no future for her here in "Oz." And yet…

"Of course I'll be back."

Dear Reader,

You asked for more ROYALLY WED titles and you've got them! For the next four months we've brought back the Stanbury family—first introduced in a short story by Carla Cassidy on our eHarlequin.com Web site. Be sure to check the archives to find Nicholas's story! But don't forget to pick up Stella Bagwell's *The Expectant Princess* and discover the involving story of the disappearance of King Michael.

Other treats this month include Marie Ferrarella's one hundredth title for Silhouette Books! This wonderful, charming and emotional writer shows her trademark warmth and humor in *Rough Around the Edges*. Luckily for all her devoted readers, Marie has at least another hundred plots bubbling in her imagination, and we'll be seeing more from her in many of our Silhouette lines.

Then we've got Karen Rose Smith's *Tall, Dark & True* about a strong, silent sheriff who can't bear to keep quiet about his feelings any longer. And Donna Clayton's heroine asks *Who Will Father My Baby?*—and gets a surprising answer. *No Place Like Home* by Robin Nicholas is a delightful read that reminds us of an all-time favorite movie—I'll let you guess which one! And don't forget first-time author Roxann Delaney's debut title, *Rachel's Rescuer*.

Next month be sure to return for *The Blacksheep Prince's Bride* by Martha Shields, the next of the ROYALLY WED series. Also returning are popular authors Judy Christenberry and Elizabeth August.

Happy reading!

Mary-Theresa Hussey

Mary-Theresa Hussey
Senior Editor

Please address questions and book requests to:
Silhouette Reader Service
U.S.: 3010 Walden Ave., P.O. Box 1325, Buffalo, NY 14269
Canadian: P.O. Box 609, Fort Erie, Ont. L2A 5X3

No Place
Like Home

ROBIN NICHOLAS

SILHOUETTE *Romance*®

Published by Silhouette Books

America's Publisher of Contemporary Romance

If you purchased this book without a cover you should be aware
that this book is stolen property. It was reported as "unsold and
destroyed" to the publisher, and neither the author nor the
publisher has received any payment for this "stripped book."

May you find your heart's desire

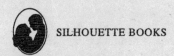 SILHOUETTE BOOKS

ISBN 0-373-19508-7

NO PLACE LIKE HOME

Copyright © 2001 by Robin Kapala

All rights reserved. Except for use in any review, the reproduction
or utilization of this work in whole or in part in any form by any
electronic, mechanical or other means, now known or hereafter
invented, including xerography, photocopying and recording, or in
any information storage or retrieval system, is forbidden without
the written permission of the editorial office, Silhouette Books,
300 East 42nd Street, New York, NY 10017 U.S.A.

All characters in this book have no existence outside the imagination of
the author and have no relation whatsoever to anyone bearing the same
name or names. They are not even distantly inspired by any individual
known or unknown to the author, and all incidents are pure invention.

This edition published by arrangement with Harlequin Books S.A.

® and TM are trademarks of Harlequin Books S.A., used under license.
Trademarks indicated with ® are registered in the United States Patent
and Trademark Office, the Canadian Trade Marks Office and in other
countries.

Visit Silhouette at www.eHarlequin.com

Printed in U.S.A.

Books by Robin Nicholas

Silhouette Romance

The Cowboy and His Lady #1017
Wrangler's Wedding #1049
Man, Wife and Little Wonder #1301
Cowboy Dad #1327
No Place Like Home #1508

ROBIN NICHOLAS

lives in Illinois with her husband, Dan, and their son, Nick. Her debut book, *The Cowboy and His Lady*, was part of the successful Silhouette Romance CELEBRATION 1000! promotion. And her third book, *Man, Wife and Little Wonder*, was Silhouette Romance's featured BUNDLES OF JOY title.

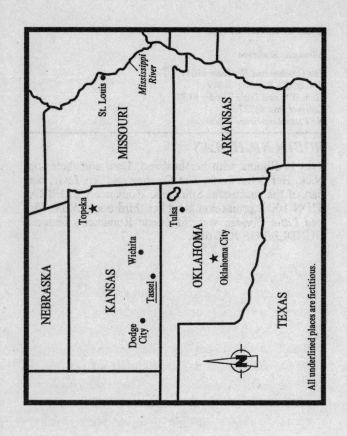

All underlined places are fictitious.

Chapter One

There was nothing like knowing she *had* to do something to trigger the stubborn side of Mariah Morgan's normally outgoing nature.

Such was the case, as, south of the Kansas/Oklahoma border and several miles west of Highway 35, she opened the door to the dubious ambience of rundown Trixie's Café. The vanity plates, STRMY F5, on the mud-splattered 4×4 sport utility truck parked outside told her she'd finally tracked down the elusive, reclusive "Stormy" Taylor. But instead of feeling relieved, she struggled with resentment.

A feature on the storm photographer could save her job at *Plain View Magazine*—so her editor said of her "lackluster work" of late. But she found it hard to get excited over a story on a thirty-five-year-old who chased tornadoes for a living. Only an ingrained aversion to poverty had brought her here.

A hot, dusty breeze trailed her through the door, tugging wisps of her curly, dark hair from its tidy bun. Slinging her purse strap over the shoulder of her royal blue short suit, she shut the door resolutely, sealing in an onslaught of onions and coffee. Conversation came in bursts laced with adjectives like snaky and hellish, and terms like vortex and dryline, all from an unkempt group who looked more than capable of chasing down tornadoes.

All eyes turned her way and talk ceased abruptly, save for the husky voice of a tawny-haired man seated at the far end of the counter. His wrinkled field shirt hung loose of his jeans, his back turned to her as he continued to drawl sexily into the cell phone he held to his ear.

"You know how to reach me, sweetheart. Just be waiting."

There came a pause during which he seemed to notice the quiet. Half turning on the creaky stool he slouched on, he zeroed sharp hazel eyes on her as the cause of the sudden silence. His gaze turned cautious yet aware as he spoke succinctly into the phone. "Later, sweetheart."

Mariah flushed hotly as he pocketed the phone. The responsive flutter in the pit of her stomach annoyed her. Only one kind of man eyed a woman that way when he was talking to his sweetheart.

She turned her attention to the group occupying the table in the center of the café, wondering which one was Stormy—the burly old man in coveralls, the dark-haired devil using a laptop or one of two slender young men who looked like they belonged on safari. Realizing she'd have done better to blend with this group clad in khaki and denim, she envisioned herself in her Levi's and forced a smile.

"Hello. I'm Mariah Morgan from the Wichita office of *Plain View Magazine*. I noticed the plates on the white truck outside and wondered if one of you folks might be Stormy Taylor."

Eyebrows raised. Skeptical glances were exchanged. No one offered a word.

Then a husky voice drawled from behind her, "I'm Rafe Taylor."

Mariah clenched her jaw. Hanging on to her smile with effort, she faced those assessing eyes once more. "Mr. Taylor."

The occupants of the table behind her snickered.

"Rafe will do."

"Rafe, then." She would remain gracious; she

preferred gracious to groveling, which was probably closer to the truth, all things considered. He hadn't responded to any messages she'd left him at his headquarters in some obscure little map dot in southwest Kansas called Tassel. His secretary had finally deigned to take her call, only to send her on this goose chase to track him down—an obvious ploy to discourage her. The death of his wife during a tornado last spring, leaving him with a daughter to raise, had apparently triggered an animosity for all journalists, not just those who went after his tragic story. With a confidence she didn't feel, she continued, "Your secretary helped me locate you."

Another round of snickers ensued, which Rafe silenced with a wry glance.

...*eight...nine...ten.* Mariah exhaled and continued again. "As I told your friends, I'm from *Plain View Magazine.* We'd like to do a feature regarding your work as a storm photographer."

"Why?"

Why? Most people didn't care why. They just wanted to be written up in a magazine. Heaven only knew what it would take to tempt this man who obviously despised journalists. Striving for professionalism, she quoted, "Editors at *Plain View* believe your occupation appeals to human interest, thus enabling us to entertain readers while at the same time raising their awareness of the dangers of—"

"What do *you* believe?"

Feeling suddenly transparent, her jaw aching with tension, she said tightly, "Pardon me?"

"Why do *you* want to write this feature?"

Because if I don't, my job will vanish, as surely as if one of your tornadoes swept it away. Mariah swallowed, her throat dry as Kansas dust. "Perhaps you'll let me buy you lunch while I explain what the ed—what I have in mind."

She thought he might refuse. She could see it in his eyes, in the stubborn thrust of his unshaven jaw. He was a handsome rogue, with an almost sultry sulky mouth and high cheekbones buffed by wind and sun. His brown hair shone as if in sunlight, some crisply cut strands standing on end—more a reflection of his impatience than the wind, she imagined. But it was her fingers, not his, that she envisioned pushing through the silky looking strands....

A cup clattered atop the counter, making her jump.

"Here's your coffee, Stormy. Now quit harassing my customer and let her sit down."

Trixie, Mariah surmised, flashing the small but sturdy woman behind the counter a grateful smile. Rafe shrugged his acquiescence, rising slightly from his stool in a faint show of manners. She'd bet there wasn't an ounce of fat hidden beneath his rumpled shirt, his body lean and long, his jeans stretched taut over his muscled thighs. Mariah slipped onto the stool beside him, her black pumps tangling with his dusty hiking boots, her gaze locked with his for an electric moment before he sat, too. Hooking her heels on the rungs of the stool, she placed her purse on the counter, battling another irritating round of flutters.

"What'll you have, miss?" Their hostess waved her hand dismissively at Rafe. "He's already eaten."

Taking an immediate liking to the denim-clad woman with her firm drawl, coffee-brown eyes and shoe-polish-black cropped hair, Mariah smiled. "I'd like iced tea and a BLT."

"White or wheat?"

"Wheat, please." She turned to ask politely if Rafe cared for anything, only to find his attention turned to the dark-haired devil at the table, who'd slipped on a headphone. Rafe seemed to wait for some sign as the man listened intently, obviously tuning out the conversation that had picked up around him.

Mariah took the moment to study Rafe. He didn't strike her as crazy, as he was purported to be, following some of his risky chases. Despite the unholy gleam she'd seen in his eyes, he seemed intelligent, a deliberate type, diligent in his quest for…storms. Mariah sighed. There was just no getting around the fact that the man chased storms for a living, an absurdity she had to showcase on paper.

Trixie set a glass of iced tea on the counter and, murmuring a thank you, Mariah turned dismally to it, stirring in extra sugar from small pink packets on the counter. She was tired and hungry and more than a little discouraged. She hadn't been sleeping well lately. After a restless night, she'd left Wichita, driving a hundred miles in search of "Stormy" Taylor, to write a story she didn't want to write in order to save a job that her thoughts hadn't centered around of late.

The scrape of a chair from a corner of the café drew her attention. A small boy, clad in an oversize T-shirt and baggy, denim shorts, climbed to a standing position on the chair and fed a quarter into an ancient pinball machine, putting a ball in play. He was cute, maybe six, with a mop of black hair that made her suspect he belonged to Trixie. It seemed she was always noticing kids these days. Probably because her sister and brother-in-law, who lived in Kansas City, had a baby on the way. Her brother and his wife in California already had three sons. The twinge of envy that accompanied her thoughts had become familiar. Turning thirty, with no husband in sight, apparently left a woman susceptible to such feelings.

The game ended abruptly. The boy stood forlornly on the chair, stirring her sympathy. Having grown up the poor kid on the block, she knew all too well what he felt like. When the quarter was gone, it was gone.

Which served to remind her why she'd chosen to write the story of her career about "Stormy." She turned to face Rafe, only to find him studying *her,* as if he had his camera in hand, contemplating a portrait. Mariah froze, unblinking, acutely conscious of their knees brushing, of her face turned up to his.

"Ever seen a tornado?" he asked, the way one might ask if she'd ever seen a rainbow.

But there was a gleam of challenge in his eyes that put her on the defensive, that reminded her he was a journalist, too. "My mother always made me go into the basement when there was a tornado coming."

Her sarcasm had Rafe chuckling before he could stop himself, a fact his fellow chasers didn't miss, judging by the second silence from the table behind him. That she'd categorized him as an "outlaw" who chased only for the thrill was obvious. But it didn't take a professional chaser to spot the storm brewing in Mariah's pretty blue eyes. They were downright turbulent. Though when she'd watched Trixie's boy, they'd gone soft and gentle, in that way a woman's eyes softened only for a child.

At least, most women. His wife, Ann, had proved to be in a class all her own. He'd known and loved her all of his life, thought his dreams had come true when she'd loved him back. Sunny had come along before he'd realized that Ann had seen him, and the notoriety that came with his profession, as her ticket out of Tassel. She'd craved media attention as much as he'd come to despise it.

He'd made clear that for him, there was no place like home. Now he had to live with the guilty secret that Ann had been leaving him—and Sunny— the night she was killed. Getting past that guilt wasn't easy with the press continually dredging up the story of her death. He was determined to shield Sunny from those trying to capitalize on his personal life.

Although, he had to admit, Mariah wasn't sending out the usual greedy vibes. She seemed downright reluctant, maybe even resentful to be here. He cocked his head. "How come I get the impression you didn't raise your hand for this assignment?"

Color rose in her cheeks. In her sophisticated clothes and hairdo he'd put her close to thirty, but she seemed very young in that moment, silky curls frizzing about her face, a dash of golden freckles showing through the dusting of powder on her pert nose. But the blush quickly gave way to that determination he'd come to expect from those seeking his story.

"I'm sorry if I gave that impression." She held his gaze firmly. "I can assure you I'll do my professional best if you'll grant me two weeks of your time for an in-depth interview."

Two weeks?

His comrades seated at the table had quieted again. He could feel their gazes trained on his back with the same intensity they applied to the sky. Stormy Taylor didn't give interviews anymore, but they apparently sensed a change in the atmosphere.

They were wrong. The lady herself might be tempting, but the "in-depth" interview wasn't. He rose from his seat, careful to keep from brushing against her silk-clad legs. "Sorry. But I'm not interested."

"But you haven't even considered—"

"I don't need to." He leaned near her to warn, "I won't have my daughter reliving the pain of her mother's death again through Mariah Morgan's point of view."

He could see the temper flash in her eyes, like a lightning strike. He could see each dark, curling lash. He'd lost track of position, gotten too close, the supreme mistake of curious chasers.

"*Plain View* is *not* a tabloid, and *I* am not a tabloid journalist."

"That's what they all say." He stepped back, intending to join his chase partner, Jeremy, at the table. But Trixie's boy, Jess, came running from the pinball machine, blocking his escape.

"Hey, Stormy. You goin' on a chase?"

Acutely aware Mariah listened, he said noncommittally, "Could be."

"Jess, come around here and fill these sugar bowls," Trixie directed her son. Then she added pointedly, "Stormy doesn't have time to answer questions today."

"Aw, Mom." Jess rolled his eyes and plodded around the counter, climbing onto the stool his mother pulled up for him. Rafe felt like rolling his eyes, too, but Trixie would be burning his steaks for a month if he did. She could usually be counted on to run interference for him, but for some reason, she'd left him at Mariah's mercy. Probably sworn off men again. Come to think of it, she'd burned Jeremy's steak today....

Deciding not to meddle with those particular forces of nature, both women glaring at him now, he strode to the table and leaned over to study the data on Jeremy's laptop.

But it was hard to concentrate with Trixie frowning at him, Jess pouting and Mariah turning her back to sit stiffly facing the counter, making him feel like he'd made it rain on their picnic.

He refused to feel guilty over turning down yet another risk to his daughter's well-being. As Mariah focused her attention on Jess and his bowls of sugar, Rafe peered closer at the Doppler image that appeared on the screen.

These past three days, they'd chased storms over western Texas and into Oklahoma, making their way to Jeremy's home base, a rundown farmhouse near the café. Now chances looked ripe for late-afternoon storms. They needed to check the data, try to narrow their target area.

But the forecast failed to hold his attention when Jess giggled and Mariah laughed; an unaffected laugh that told him she'd momentarily forgotten her mission—namely *him*. He watched a packet of sugar being exchanged from Jess's small hand to Mariah's pretty crimson-polished fingers.

"The National Weather Service just issued a storm watch extending from central Oklahoma up into south central Nebraska. North central Kansas is ranked a high-risk zone." Jeremy grinned as he drawled out the report, his dark eyes lit with excitement, as if he was sitting in paradise instead of Tornado Alley's hot zone.

Rafe knew that for Jeremy, chase fever, which struck before the primary chase season of mid-April to mid-June, was a permanent condition. He was as close to being an outlaw chaser as Rafe was far from it since the birth of his child. Having a daughter had changed Rafe's approach to his work for the better. Until lately...

Rafe knew his photos had made a difference in the study of storms that spawned killer tornadoes. That had been the purpose of his career. But the chase had taken on a different meaning since Ann's death. He was taking risks he didn't normally take, aware that each storm he "captured" on film gave Sunny a better understanding of the tornado that had claimed her mother's life, helping Sunny to cope with her loss and her resulting fear of storms.

Mariah shot a furtive glance over her shoulder, no doubt sensing a story in the air. He kept his voice low. "We're within striking distance if we leave now."

Their fellow chasers, two impatient young college men aiming for careers in meteorology, and Gus, an old farmer who'd served as a weather spotter for years, had already scooted back their chairs. The college boys left in a whirlwind of khaki, not about to miss any action. Gus planned to go home and warn his wife of fifty years; she liked to tag along when he chased.

Jeremy moved into action, deftly disassembling his equipment. At the counter, Mariah dug bills out of her purse, tucking a twenty under a corner of the untouched plate Trixie had brought her. She slipped a dollar to Jess, and Rafe smiled reluctantly. But when Mariah's gaze met his, he pursed his lips, straightening from the table. "The dryline looks to merge right on top of Highway 281."

Jeremy's eyes gleamed as he rose. "We should drive right into the son of a gun."

"Let's go." Rafe was grimly aware of Mariah hitching her purse over her shoulder, scooting her small butt off the stool, ready to chase him down as surely as he'd chase a tornado.

Jeremy called out to Trixie, "We've got weather coming this afternoon. You and Jess be ready to take shelter."

"*I* know what to do," Trixie shot back at him.

With no doubt that Trixie would look after Mariah if need be, Rafe nudged Jeremy out of a staredown with the stubborn café owner. Jeremy would have better luck facing down a tornado. As for himself, he wasn't going to get caught face-to-face with pretty Mariah again.

He reached the door first, pulling it open. Jeremy

pushed through with his equipment, the competitive edge still there, no matter that they were partners, gathering photos for a stock photography agency. Rafe followed him out, digging keys from his pocket, exchanging a round of "keep in touch" and "watch your backside." They'd each find their own route, seeking storms based on their own forecasting quirks, converging later in the vicinity of the largest storm.

Jeremy climbed in a battered black pickup that often served as a second home. Rafe curled his hand around the chrome handle of his truck's door, adrenaline kicking in. A strong jet stream moved this storm. He wasn't going home tonight without "capturing" a tornado on film for his daughter.

"Wait!"

Impatient, he glanced back all the same when Mariah called out from the café door. She jogged toward him, gravel scarring her leather heels, her purse dangling by its strap from her hand. He grimaced. Anything for the story.

In a sense, he understood; he'd reached the point where he would do almost anything for a picture. Since she'd failed to win his cooperation, he suspected Mariah would resort to the ultimate threat, the way they all did, warning him that she would write her own version of his personal past if he didn't reveal the facts.

The sun-heated chrome burned hot against his palm, the need to protect his daughter churning through him. Jeremy gunned his pickup, fishtailing by with a grin and raising a cloud of gravel dust. Rafe muttered a curse and yanked open the truck door. He wasn't waiting around—

He drew up short, Mariah suddenly wedged between his hip and the truck seat, blocking his slide in. She squinted up at him, the sky still a deceptive baby blue—kind of like her innocent eyes.

He braced himself for the threat, or maybe even a bribe.

But her gaze turned dark and desperate, her voice low and gritty as she told him, "If I don't get this story, I'll be fired."

Chapter Two

Time hung suspended on the hot, dusty air between them, Rafe weighing the consequences of physically moving Mariah from his path so he could climb into his truck to chase a storm he instinctively knew would be less threatening.

A light, sweet scent lifted from her skin, wafting through the heat and the grit. With his next breath, he knew the consequences would be high. He kept his hands to himself, determined to turn down her request for his time—and his story.

But the refusal wouldn't come. He kept picturing her inside the café, giving Jess a dollar, tipping Trixie a twenty for her trouble, all the while aware she'd just lost the interview that would save her job. Even knowing the threat posed by the desperation in her eyes, he couldn't bring himself to turn her away.

"All right, get in. But I'm not promising anything."

She turned in the small space between them, tossing her purse on the truck seat. Rafe sucked in a breath, leaning back in a halfhearted effort to give her more room. Then she was pressing her hand to his chest, her bright crimson nails seeming to burn through his drab field shirt.

"I'll be right back—I have to get my things."

She edged by with a brush of curls and silk and curves. Rafe exhaled, bracing his free hand atop the truck.

A chase required precision forecasting and an eye to the elements. Only the merging of specific atmospheric elements and events at the same time could form the kind of storms that produced tornadoes. And only perfect timing on his part would put him in the right location for a photograph.

Mariah promised to thoroughly distract him.

Even now, she leaned inside her rental coupe, her flirty shorts hiked up her silk covered thighs. Rafe grimaced. Who would have thought a *journalist* would be the one to stir his hormones back to life?

She straightened, her arms filled with electronic

gear—a laptop, a tape recorder, a cell phone. The lady meant business, he realized grimly. He hauled himself into the truck, her little black purse occupying the passenger seat. He ought to toss it out and drive off. As she started over, Mariah's wary gaze met his, as if she suspected he might do just that.

Then it was too late. She deposited her gear atop her purse, scrambling in with a flash of leg. Rafe thrust her things in back with his equipment. Buckling her seat belt, she said breathlessly, "Ready."

Gravel sprayed from beneath the truck's wheels as he shot out of the parking lot.

Mariah clutched at the dash, disturbing neatly rolled maps, earning a frown from Rafe. She straightened them, sinking into the bucket seat.

At least he drove reasonably near the speed limit. Panning the endless blue sky for clouds, her focus suddenly narrowed. On the passenger side, tape had been placed in a "X" over a star cracked into the bug-splattered windshield. Dents riddled the hood. Hail? she wondered. What kind of storm produced hail large enough to cause that much damage? An image of the truck's mud-crusted wheel wells registered in her mind. Considering Rafe's reputation for risk taking, joining him on a chase seemed foolish in retrospect.

But she had a job at stake.

Putting herself at ease the best way she knew how, she perused the truck's interior. Video camera mounted on the dash, radios, scanners, even a TV monitor. She peered between the seats. He'd apparently gutted the back for storage.

Awareness tingled through her, triggered by an earthy scent she recognized as Rafe's. His shirtsleeve grazed her cheek; his body heat warmed her. A glance revealed the clench of his stubbled jaw. Unfamiliar as she was with meteorology, Mariah recognized the charged atmosphere between them. She eased back into her seat.

And she proceeded to grill him on his interesting array of equipment, right down to the cell phone she knew he carried in his pocket.

"So, you're saying your cell phone system interfaces with your laptop for on-road reports?"

"That's right."

A man of few words. "What about that oddlooking instrument mounted outside? Not the antennas, but the staff with the three little cups attached?"

"The anemometer. Measures wind speed."

She attempted a closer look out the window, pushing at the creeping hem of her shorts. "How does it work? Do the cups rotate—"

"Yes. They do. Just…sit back. I need to…listen to the radio for NWS reports."

More curious than apprehensive now, Mariah caught her lip. Then she asked, "What's NWS?"

"The National Weather Service. Look, this isn't Tornado Tours."

"They give *tours* to see tornadoes?"

"That's it! No more questions. Just…study the map."

He thrust "Kansas" into her lap. Mariah slumped in the seat, chastened by his tone. She'd bet Stormy "Charisma" Taylor didn't pad his income giving tours.

He'd apparently meant it when he said no promises. Well, he'd underestimated her determination. She was part of this chase, no matter how he tried to shut her out. Before the day was over, he'd be so convinced of her sincerity regarding his absurd career, he'd be *begging* her to write the feature.

But concentrating on the map she spread over her lap quickly proved unnecessary; how much expertise did it require to drive straight up 281? And watching the sky seemed pointless when there wasn't a cloud in sight. Chasing storms apparently involved a lot of driving in perfectly lovely weather. Mariah stifled a yawn, wondering if his reputation, like that of so many famed personalities, was more fiction than fact.

When he finally spotted a storm, she supposed he would stop and wait for a tornado to form in the distance, then take a picture. After all, this wasn't the movies. She'd seen news footage of what happened to fools with video cameras who got too close to storms. You didn't drive right up to a tornado and take photographs in real life. That was what zoom lenses were created for.

Mariah absently folded the edge of the map with her fingers, only to smooth it when she caught Rafe's frown. Sighing, she slid farther down in the seat, heedless of her tidy bun. As she gazed through the windshield, past the taped-over crack, the clear line of the horizon blurred. Even in the company of a handsome man, chasing storms was actually quite boring....

Mariah stirred in the warm cocoon of her blanket, breathing deeply of a fragrance she'd come to savor, an earthy scent that triggered a basic need deep within her—

She stilled, hiding behind lowered lashes. She wasn't in bed. This wasn't her blanket she'd just curled her fingers into, a button poking into her palm. The heat encompassing her came from the body invading her space. And the earthy scent she breathed wasn't fragrance, it was *Rafe.*

Mariah blinked and gazed into Rafe's startled eyes.

He leaned over her, perilously near, his weight braced on his hand atop the seat, the tail of his field shirt grazing her silk-covered knees. The heat of him seemed to press upon her, intensified by the glow that came into his eyes. The glow deepened to a burn and expectation shivered through her. He was going to *kiss* her....

Mariah closed her eyes as he settled his mouth over hers, a soft touch that reached deep. With the rasp of his whiskery jaw and the warmth of his breath on her skin, longing rose within her, had her pressing her lips against his. A kaleidoscope of color whirled behind her closed lids, his kiss stealing her breath, that same mix of awe and apprehension she'd experienced facing the storm spinning through her. Helpless, she felt her heart race as he blew her away with his kiss.

His mouth left hers, his shirt tugging against her clenched fingers. Mariah opened her eyes, her pulse pounding as he hovered over her. Yearning speared through her. She realized now the extent to which she'd neglected her sexual side in her quest for a career.

Rafe's breath rushed out. "I didn't mean to do that."

Her face burned. She let go of his shirt. "Neither did I. Let's just forget it happened."

"Deal."

Deal? Mariah curled her hand in a fist. Maybe he'd like her to sign a contract, too?

"I need my camera." He pressed close again, reaching past her to open a cupboard in the back of the truck. She suffered the near choke hold of his muscled arm, his dusty shirt falling across her face. Settling into his seat, he adjusted the settings on a still camera. "I have to scout out a place to shoot from."

He climbed out of the truck, shut the door and left her frowning after him, still feeling the effects of a kiss he'd already put behind him.

Well, she was as willing as he to ignore the kiss *he'd* stolen. She was especially willing to overlook the fact that she'd kissed him back.

Locating a clock among his myriad gadgets, she realized she'd wasted almost two hours sleeping. *Kissing.*

At some point, he'd left the highway for a north-bound gravel road. Getting out to stand on the grassy shoulder, she noticed "Kansas" was no longer spread over her lap, the map rolled neatly on the dash once more. Rafe must have slipped it from her hands while she was asleep.

Recalling the startled look in his eyes, she realized he hadn't intended to wake her at all.

She gritted her teeth. He hadn't intended to wake her, but he'd been willing to *kiss* her when she did.

Stiffening her travel-weary legs, she trudged to the back of the truck, where Rafe was in the process of unlocking the hatchback. She gave him a lethal glare. "You could have wakened me."

Then she ducked as he raised the door.

"Sorry. I'm kind of busy right now." He pulled out a tripod with a video camera mounted on top. Hefting it to his shoulder, he lowered the hatch, brushing by her to hurry up the roadside slope.

Mariah hiked after him. Dry weeds tugged at her sheer stockings. *Silk* stockings. She wondered if they were an accountable expense.

Rafe stationed the tripod halfway up the knoll, fiddling with the video camera. Curiosity overrode her pique. Brushing back wispy curls the breeze blew across her cheek, she queried, "What, exactly, are you doing?"

He straightened from behind the camera and gave her a pointed look. But she couldn't help it. Her mother claimed she'd been born asking questions.

"I'm trying to align the viewfinder. Could you step out of the way, please?"

"I don't see what the rush is." She tilted her

face to the sky, a scattering of fluffy white clouds floating by.

He stepped from behind the camera, looming over her for a moment during which his height was imprinted on her mind. Then he grasped her by the shoulders and turned her to face the northern sky. "In case you haven't noticed, there's a storm moving by."

For a moment she didn't notice; there was only the heat of his strong hands cupping her shoulders, obliterating even the perpetual Kansas wind in her face. All she could think was that she wanted him to kiss her again. The way his hands lingered told her he wanted it, too.

A strong sense of self-preservation made her focus intently on the distant storm. Though acutely aware when he took his hands from her, she drew a breath of surprise at the panorama building before her.

"Oh my." A few miles to the north an explosion of pure white cloud billowed in high puffed layers. Beneath the mass, varying shades from greenish-gray to dark blue, from glistening white to black, extended from the northeast reaches to the southwest edges of the storm. "It's beautiful."

"I wouldn't mind getting a picture of it," Rafe said dryly. She faced him with a determination meant to convey she was here to stay. He'd already raised his still camera, shooting away. Seemingly at *her*.

Mariah moved hastily out of range, conscious of her windblown hair, wrinkled clothes and run stockings. There was obviously no use in talking to him now. He fired off that camera like an automatic weapon, going through a roll of film in less than a minute, trading it for a fresh roll from his pocket, reloading and shooting again.

The storm was indeed a magnificent sight moving across the prairie, more imposing than when viewed from the confines of the city. Yet she felt that same safe feeling she'd felt as a child, watching the rain from the shelter of her parents' front porch. With Rafe standing between her and the approaching front, broad-shouldered and enlightened to any danger, it was easy to understand where that sense of security came from.

Her untrained eye began to distinguish the storm darkening as it traveled in a northeasterly direction. Questions gathered in her mind as he captured the scene on film. But he seemed to have forgotten she was there.

He already regretted her presence; rather than interrupt him, Mariah took a moment to survey her surroundings. Behind her, the land rose, leveling off at a barbed-wire fence. Cropped pastures lined the roadsides, and she wondered if there were cows grazing up there. Or maybe even a horse. Like most females, she was drawn by the equine mystique.

Lightning crackled in the distance. Mariah flinched, glancing over her shoulder. Rafe's back was to her, his camera aimed at the flashes that streaked the sky. If she found a horse and rode away, he wouldn't notice until he ran out of film.

Calmed by his lack of alarm, she climbed to the top of the knoll and curled her hands around the fence.

Disappointment swept through her. Not a horse in sight. Not even a cow, though evidence of them lay in pungent dried chips on the ground.

The breeze seemed stronger at the top of the slope and felt good on her skin after the climb. Goose bumps pricked her arms, tingled her scalp—

Rafe reached around her, closing his hands overtop of hers, prying her fingers from the wire. Before she could protest, he swung her away from the fence. Jagged bolts dropped from the clouds, effectively closing the miles between them and the storm. Thunder reverberated, but failed to drown out his curse—likely over the picture he'd just missed. He ushered her down the weedy slope to where he'd set up the video camera, and her temper flared with each step she took.

He faced her abruptly, grasping her arms as if

tempted to shake some sense into her. "Are you *crazy?* If lightning strikes that wire, even *miles* away, you might as well grab hold of a power line! *Always* keep your distance from a fence in a storm."

"Well, *excuse me.* But I don't chase storms for a living."

"I know. Your mother sends you to the basement."

She glared at him and his hands tightened on her arms. Then they gentled. Cold then hot, he was as changing as the weather. Mariah shivered; she felt the heat. But she couldn't help wondering if the scare she'd given him had turned his thoughts to Ann.

The breeze buffeted their bodies against each other and abruptly, he released her.

"Just…stay by me, okay? I need to get some more pictures."

He didn't like that he wanted her. And she liked it too much. But he clearly felt responsible for her well-being, if only because he was stuck with her.

Surprisingly, as he resumed shooting, he offered a grudging explanation from behind the camera. "That dark cloud close to the ground, beneath the center of the updraft base, is a wall cloud."

Updraft base? Wall cloud? Intrigued, she followed him, edging along the roadside in the direction of the storm. "The wide one with the rather jagged looking edges?"

"That's right."

"The one kind of…hovering there?"

"Yeah…"

"The one kind of…churning?"

"Rotating… Damn." Rafe lowered the camera. "It's started to rotate."

"That's what I said. And just feel that cool fresh air." Standing beside him, Mariah breathed deeply of the rich country scent, the invigorating breeze combining with Rafe's more cooperative mood to perk up her spirit. She'd never thought of a storm as beautiful, but she'd like to have a picture of this one. Rafe seemed almost a part of it, the wind combing through his crisp hair, his loose shirt whipping from his lean body. His eyes seemed to reflect the electric atmosphere of the storm.

"Here." He lifted the strap from around his neck and pushed the camera into her hand. Mariah fumbled to catch hold of it, wondering if he'd read her mind. He gave her a nudge toward the truck. "Go on back. I'll be right there."

He moved swiftly toward the video camera, apparently ready to leave. She stared after him, exasperated. He did everything in such a hurry. But at least he was talking to her. On that positive note, she started down the slope, inspecting the camera, her head bent to the wind.

It looked a lot like her own 35mm at home. Mariah glanced up the knoll as Rafe hoisted the tripod to his shoulder. She caught her lip, then faced the storm, raising the camera and focusing through the viewfinder until she'd framed in the impressive wall cloud. Amazing. The storm appeared perilously closer through the eye of the camera....

"I should have made you sign a waiver," Rafe muttered from close behind, in the same moment she clicked the shutter.

"I only took one picture. I didn't break anything."

"I was thinking more along the lines of liability."

"What do you mean?" Surely they weren't in any danger. The storm was miles away, moving east.

"Never mind. Come on."

He caught her hand and pulled her the last few feet down the slope. The ground was rough along the gravelly edge of the road, and Mariah stumbled, grasping his arm for balance. The muscle beneath her hand was like iron. Tense. She glanced up at him. His jaw was set, his mouth pressed grimly, his mind clearly on the business of packing up.

Mariah moved back as he opened the hatch to store the tripod. She stepped slowly from behind the truck, breeze flowing over her, along with a sense of unreality as she surveyed the storm. The beauty of the massive white clouds seemed suddenly eclipsed by the sinister air of the wall cloud, the blackish-blue mass churning faster, holding her mesmerized. The branches of a nearby cottonwood bowed and cold air rushed over her skin. She should have been frightened. But when the snaky gray funnel dropped from the cloud, she instinctively raised the camera.

"Mariah!"

Rafe's voice came faintly from behind her, the wind whipping her name away. He wouldn't like it if she used up his film…. She stared through the viewfinder, entranced as the funnel touched down.

"*The Wizard of Oz* tornado…" she murmured.

Click. The base darkened—with dust and debris, she realized. And it was coming closer….

She lowered the camera, eyes wide.

"Mariah!" Rafe gripped her arm, hauling her toward the truck door despite the fact that her legs didn't seem to work. "You're crazier than Jeremy! Get in!"

He hustled her inside. The wind beat at him as he rounded the truck, dust swirling, making him shield his eyes with his hand. He yanked open the door and shot onto the seat. Firing the engine, he swung the truck in a U-turn, skidding out of it to tear down the road, spraying gravel.

Mariah drew a choked breath at the sight of the churning funnel through the rear window, and her sense of unreality effectively vanished. But Rafe had only to keep heading south and they would drive out of the storm.

"We've got a right mover, Jeremy," Rafe shouted into the CB mike. "I'm on a gravel road, west of 281. Are you in the path of the storm?"

Jeremy's voice crackled over the airwaves, barely distinguishable as he transmitted. "...road ends...get the hell out—"

For Mariah, the last was clear enough.

"Hang on!"

She gripped the dash as Rafe turned the wheel sharply, heading east on a strip of gravel—straight on a course of interception with the storm.

And he'd called *her* crazy.

Had he actually made her feel safe from the storm? Had she actually wanted to kiss this madman?

This morning, thirty had felt old. Now it seemed *much* too young to die.

Mariah flinched, a cottonwood branch skidding across the truck's hood. Her imagination, never lacking, conjured vivid images of what else the tornado had sucked up and sent spinning—plant life, homes, the people in them.

Ann Taylor.

How could Rafe take these risks after the death of his wife? His daughter depended on him. He was nothing like the responsible family men her father, brother and brother-in-law were. Not at all the kind of man she should want to kiss.

The next gust shrouded the road before them with thick dust, dragging against the truck until it seemed to crawl. A dark wall of rain closed in, slashed with lightning and rimmed with streaks of bright white. Relief left her weak. "The tornado is gone! Vanished! There's only rain now!"

"It isn't gone," Rafe said tersely. "We just can't see it. And that isn't just rain. It's a hailstorm."

A tornado they couldn't see. Like some invisible stalker. And hail. Somehow she suspected it wouldn't be the tiny stones she used to collect from the sidewalk after a summer rain.

The first drops fell, a light rain that grew louder as hailstones littered the road and ricocheted off the hood. They came harder and faster, like her heartbeat.

Rafe dragged a blanket up between the seats. "Cover up, in case the windshield takes a hit."

How would Rafe protect himself? She'd raised

the thick quilt to her shoulders when a large stone struck the glass with a resounding crack. Dropping the blanket, she snatched tape from the dash, ripping off strips and slapping them across the new star in the window, stemming the flow of rain-washed air. Wind rammed the truck, a jarring reminder of the lurking tornado. They could die— and in that moment, all she could think was how she'd never had a child.

"Hang on!"

Rafe swung the truck in a southbound turn onto 281 and floored the gas pedal. Within moments, the hail stopped. The rain let up. A mile later, they'd driven from beneath the dark canopy of clouds, the skies lightening, the wind lessening to a breeze. Mariah searched for the tornado, but there was only the dark storm rotating across the prairie, leaving a broken trail behind.

Rafe stopped the truck, killing the engine. Her heart pounded in the silence. Gold-tipped fields of winter wheat waved gently on the roadsides in soft sunlight.

"You okay?" Rafe gripped her shoulders, his gaze delving into her eyes. A life-affirming awareness pulsed between them. Then he released her, pulling the blanket from her grip, tossing it to the rear. "I'd better survey the damage."

The closing of the truck door jolted her. A delayed trembling shook her, the nearness of their brush with disaster striking her anew. They'd almost been *killed.*

And it was all his fault.

Mariah pushed out of the truck, tromping around front in her scarred shoes and tattered stockings. The flow of clean, damp air over dusty ground and dry pavement only heightened her awareness of nature's unpredictable power. Ignoring the curls that frizzed across her face, she vented her emotions in a shaky voice. "This is all your fault."

Rafe straightened from the smashed headlight he examined. "We're safe now. And if I remember right, it was *your* idea to come along."

His calm after the storm infuriated her. "You almost got us killed!"

Frowning, he twisted off the remains of a broken antenna. "Another way you might look at it is that I saved both our a—"

Mariah knocked the antenna from his hand. "I think you drove us into that storm just to scare me."

His angry gaze bore into hers. "I drove us *out* of that storm the only way I could. We had a close call, but believe me, it could have been worse."

"All in a day's work?"

"That's right."

The sun burned over them, warming already

heated tempers, fueling underlying sparks before Rafe turned away, continuing a post-storm inspection she suspected he made on a regular basis. He was probably already planning his next chase.

And she wanted no part of it. Her near brush with death had come with a revelation. She knew why she wasn't sleeping at night, why her work was lackluster, why she noticed children everywhere. She wanted a child, and a dependable man to love her.

She strode to the back of the truck. Her gaze blazed over Rafe, who was nothing like her dear old dad or her brother. "Take me back to my car. And don't worry—I want nothing to do with writing your story."

She gave him no chance to reply, stomping back to grasp the handle on the passenger door.

Her breath caught in her throat. Rafe stood at the edge of the highway, the incessant breeze tugging his hair, his clothes. He stared after the departing storm, clearly craving to give chase again.

He *was* crazy.

And she was crazy for wanting him.

Chapter Three

All he could think about was Mariah.

Ordinarily, after a day of chasing, he'd be tired and wired, obsessing over the shots he'd taken. Instead, he was obsessing over Mariah. Over kissing Mariah...

Rafe glanced at her warily. Once again, she slept in the truck's passenger seat as he drove, deceivingly angelic with the soft evening light shining over her through the windshield. Her wind-tangled hair brought to mind the picture she'd made, framed by the backdrop of stormy sky, her dark curls blowing across her cheeks, her eyes vivid blue through the camera's viewfinder. He hadn't even noticed a tornado forming, too caught up in the sight of this woman.

He should have left her at Trixie's. But while he hadn't wanted her writing about him, he hadn't wanted to be the reason she lost her job, either. Although she'd decided not to do the feature, the truth was, he didn't trust her not to change her mind again once she discovered he was taking her home to Tassel.

How had her job come to be at risk, anyway? Despite her obvious reluctance, she'd tackled her assignment with a curiosity as dogged as that of his eight-year-old daughter. Mariah had a way of making him remember when chasing storms had been new to him, too, of making him forget, for a while, what the chase meant to him now.

As a result, he hadn't captured a tornado on film for his daughter.

The CB crackled with static. Mariah frowned in her sleep. Rafe snatched up the microphone, not about to let it disturb her. She was less trouble when she was asleep. She'd passed out this second time just after he'd radioed Jeremy to tell him they'd made it out of the storm.

An image of Mariah, her hands curled around the wire fence, bolts shooting from the heavy sky, flashed disturbingly to mind. He shook the chilling vision away as a voice came over the airwaves.

"This is Sunshine. Are you out there, Stormy?"

"That you, sweetheart?" As if he didn't know.

Storms had swept close to Tassel, too, and his daughter would want him home tonight. So he was going home.

Rafe sensed he was being observed. Sure enough, Mariah leveled her disapproving, judgmental gaze upon him—the same look she'd given him at Trixie's when he'd talked to Sunny....

Sweetheart. She thought he was talking to a woman. Considering the way he couldn't take his eyes off her at the café, and the kiss he'd stolen, he could see where she might get the wrong idea about him. Kind of like she was getting the wrong idea now.

"Of course it's me. Are you coming home, Daddy?" Sunny's aggrieved, now distinctive "kid's" voice had Mariah straightening in her seat, the judgmental look in her eyes changing to one of surprise. Rafe grimaced. Once she knew he was taking her home, she would either see the advantage of the situation and barrage him—and his family—with questions, or demand again that he drive her back to her car. He should have just wakened her and dropped her off at a roadside motel.

He raised the mike. "I'm just passing the Lightning Tree, so I'll see you real soon."

"Lightning tree?" Mariah pushed feathery curls from her cheek, peering out the window at the landmark. "I don't remember seeing a tree that had been struck by lightning."

Her tone reminded him she'd been angry he hadn't wakened her after her first nap. But he recalled it hadn't taken her long to start asking questions. Even now she was frowning, squinting into the evening sun. "I don't recall coming from the west, either."

As she craned her neck in passing at a highway sign, Rafe replaced the mike and braced himself for the inevitable.

"Highway 54—the Yellow Brick Road." Mariah murmured the nickname given the highway that led to Liberal, Kansas, home of the tourist attractions, Dorothy's House and the Land of Oz from the legendary film *The Wizard of Oz.* After today, he figured she would never view the tale of a rural Kansas girl whisked by a tornado to the Land of Oz in quite the same light. "Your headquarters in Tassel is your home, isn't it?"

Judging by her expression, he could tell she didn't know whether to be angry over being kidnapped, or amazed by her turn of luck. Best to set her straight before they got there. "I've been gone a few days and my daughter wants to see me. Don't view this as a golden opportunity and have a change of heart. I'll be taking you back to your car first thing tomorrow."

"Tomorrow? That's presumptuous of you."

But even as she said it, her journalist's mind was ruminating over the possibilities; the personal contact with Rafe's family would give her the chance to provide fact where there had only been speculation.

If she were to write the story, that is. She caught Rafe's hard, knowing gaze. Just because opportunity came knocking, that didn't mean she intended to answer. The day's close call with the harsh elements of nature had brought revelations, one of which was that he was crazy. As for herself, instead of her past flashing before her eyes, she'd beheld her future, empty and lonely without a husband and child to love. Her priorities, once centered on her career and financial security, had changed course along with the storm.

Coolly, she asked, "Did it occur to you that I might have decided to return to Wichita tonight?"

"Did you?"

There was a curious timbre to his voice, as if he wondered whether someone waited for her at home. As if he might want to kiss her again. Her answer came on a wisp of breath. "No."

"Then you can stay in our guest room tonight."

He intended for her to sleep at his house?

"I can't stay with you and your daughter. It wouldn't be appropriate." Her racing heart attested to the fact. She imagined Rafe waking her in the dark, his scent all around her, his lips on hers....

"My mother lives with us, so there shouldn't be any problem."

He lived with his *mother?* Somehow that failed to fit the image of a daredevil storm chaser. And it effectively squelched her overactive imagination.

But it was easy to conclude that his mother had come to his aid after the death of his wife left Rafe to raise his daughter on his own. She realized bleakly that his mother likely served as the secretary who had sent her on the goose chase. That qualified as a problem as far as she was concerned.

Still, she resigned herself to the arrangement, recalling the obscure little map dot that was Tassel, aware she had little option. As Rafe said, there shouldn't be any problem.

"My suitcase is locked in the rental car at Trixie's. You'll have to stop somewhere so I can buy a toothbrush."

Not to mention a few other amenities a man would never consider.

"What little there is of town closes its doors by dusk. Mom will have a spare toothbrush."

So she would endure this evening at Rafe's, with a borrowed toothbrush and no clean underwear—but only because his daughter wanted him there, Mariah thought with a welling of sympathy. Judging by the roadside puddles, she could see that storms had passed this way, as well. It was easy to understand how, after the tragic death of her mother, the child would want her father home. And, given that fact, it was impossible to understand how Rafe could continue chasing tornadoes.

He slowed the truck as they entered town, two weathered boards nailed to a post welcoming them to Tassel. A handful of quaint storefronts edged the highway, houses spread haphazardly beyond them on narrow, unlined streets. The gas station, with its two self-serve pumps, repair shop and live bait offering, was closed for the day, a Gone Fishing sign in the window. She could see clear to the west edge of town, and miles beyond in the waning light. A view that, combined with the abundance of tornadoes, made this a chaser's paradise.

At the west edge of town, Rafe turned onto a gravel lane that led to a white farmhouse. Beneath the porch eaves, lace curtains fluttered in the windows. To the east sat a neat red barn and white fence surrounding a short-grass pasture dotted with cottonwoods. The tidy homestead had a familial ambiance, most likely the lingering touch of Rafe's late wife and the preserving hand of his mother. One thing she was sure of, it owed little to Rafe.

Parked before the garage was another sturdy-looking 4×4, this one a functional blue pickup she suspected belonged to his mother. She climbed slowly from the truck, her welcome here dubious.

The screen door banged, a young girl thundering across the porch and pounding down the steps in red tennis shoes. Thick, shiny brown braids bounced at the shoulders of the white T-shirt she wore with gingham blue bib overalls. A replay of Dorothy from *The Wizard of Oz,* skipping down the Yellow Brick Road, played through Mariah's mind. Rafe rounded the truck and the child flung her arms around him, as if he'd been away from home years instead of days.

They looked her way, the girl's arms still wrapped around her father, her head resting against his middle. Her hazel eyes were the image of Rafe's, only hers were dark with mistrust while his burned with warning.

"This is my daughter, Sunny. Sunny, this is Mariah Morgan."

Sunny? Mariah was charmed, but the child clearly was not.

"I know. Grandma says she's a *journalist.*"

From Sunny's tone, Grandma might well have said she'd found a bug in the flour. Sunny looked up at her father to add confidentially, "She called here a *hundred* times."

"Sunny." Rafe frowned in exasperation.

"We don't talk about folks in front of them.

That's rude.'' The screen door swung open again, a woman with cropped silver hair, dressed in cowboy boots, jeans and a neat plaid blouse stepping outside. Slim and tall, with sharp hazel eyes, the woman's appearance, coupled with the no-nonsense twang Mariah recognized from the telephone, confirmed that Rafe's mother was also his secretary. Mariah suspected Grandma had had plenty to say about Mariah Morgan, journalist, when Mariah hadn't been around to hear it.

"Grandma's right," Rafe prodded his daughter sternly.

Sunny let go of her father. "I'm sorry, Grandma."

"I'm not the one you should say sorry to."

The girl bent to scoop up a plush gold cat that came to rub against her legs. "Sorry, Miss Morgan."

"Accepted." Although, considering Sunny's pout as she hugged her cat, Mariah suspected any contrition on the girl's part was due to disappointing her dad and her grandma. But aware of Sunny's irreplaceable loss, she could only feel compassion for the child. "Please, call me Mariah."

"Like they call the wind," Grandma said, descending the steps with a reserved smile. Dealing with the press in the aftermath of her daughter-in-law's death had clearly left her wary.

"Mariah, this is my mother, Dorothy."

Mariah tentatively returned Dorothy's smile. "Like Dorothy from *The Wizard of Oz?*"

"So my mother said." Dorothy eyed Mariah's rumpled clothes and ragged panty hose, then Rafe's battered pickup without so much as a raised brow. "I'd say you caught up with Rafe, and Rafe caught up with the weather north of here."

"We got hit with a little hail," Rafe replied easily, but the warning in his eyes burned brighter.

Naturally, he didn't want to alarm his daughter and mother with their close call, even though he hadn't considered their brush with the weather as such. His rush to escape it likely had more to do with his concern over liability, than it had respect for danger.

"NWS in Wichita reported a funnel touched down," Sunny said intently, sounding like her father and his fellow chasers. "Did you get a picture of the tornado?"

"I got some good shots of the wall cloud," Rafe said evasively. Frustration burned in his eyes and Mariah felt an irrational sense of guilt that he'd abandoned his work to get her away from the storm.

Dorothy murmured her surprise. Sunny lowered

her head, crestfallen. Without thinking, sensing the importance of the photo to Sunny, Mariah said quickly, "I took a picture of the tornado."

Three sets of hazel eyes turned upon her, Dorothy's wondering, Sunny's disbelieving, while Rafe drilled her with his gaze, making her fear she'd only managed to upset his daughter.

"*You* got a picture?" Sunny queried.

Mariah hesitated. "I'd never seen a tornado before. I was holding your father's camera. It seemed the natural thing to do."

"Dad let you use *his* camera? What did the tornado look like? Was it really an F2?"

F2? Sunny's questions whirled by faster than any tornado. At Rafe's nod, Mariah skipped to one she could readily answer. "It was…impressive. Almost white against the dark sky and spinning over green pasture."

She'd wanted to say it was beautiful, but in light of Ann's death the description didn't seem appropriate.

Sunny planted her hands on her hips. "Dad, you said there was just hail."

"There was hail—it was huge," Mariah assured her hastily. Rafe's hands were at his hips, too. "A stone cracked the windshield. I had to tape the glass to keep it from shattering while your dad drove us out of the storm."

"Sounds like you kept your head," Dorothy said on an unexpected note of approval.

Recalling the way she'd railed at Rafe in the aftermath, Mariah flushed, feeling like a fraud. But before she could confess her fear, Sunny added, "*And* she got a picture."

The child eyed her as if in a new light. But the light faded as she asked guardedly, "Are you going to use the picture in your story about my dad?"

Excruciatingly aware of Rafe, Mariah revealed, "I've decided not to write a feature on your dad."

"Why not?" Sunny probed, with the same directness as her father, questioning why she *wanted* to write his story.

She could hardly say she'd changed her mind because Rafe had scared her to death, almost getting her killed by a tornado. And she couldn't tell Sunny she didn't want to write about her father because he was crazy, that he had a dangerous career no responsible father should have.

Rafe's tension as he hovered protectively over his daughter was as tangible as the breeze across her face. Mariah chose her words with care. "I think the story requires someone more familiar with the varying aspects of the weather."

Someone who wouldn't be scared witless by hidden tornadoes and giant hailstones.

"Then why did you come home with dad?" Sunny persisted.

Because I've been kidnapped, Mariah thought wryly. But she couldn't tell Sunny that, either. Fortunately, Rafe supplied the answer. "She's here because I wanted to come see my best girl and because it's too late to make a round trip to Trixie's, where Mariah's car is parked."

"I imagine it's been a long day," Dorothy said shrewdly. "We've already eaten, but I'll heat some leftovers, then round up some fresh clothes for Mariah."

Mariah sighed over her royal blue suit. Back to wearing hand-me-downs again.

"She needs a toothbrush, too," Rafe said dryly, and she felt flustered by the faint curve of his lips and the drift of his gaze to her mouth.

"I could show you my pony while Grandma warms up your supper," Sunny offered.

"That sounds wonderful—all of it."

"My pony is in the barn," Sunny told her.

"What's his name? No, wait, let me guess." *Stormy, Sunny, Dorothy.* She decided to go with the movie theme. "Oz? Like *The Wizard of Oz?*"

"This old tomcat is Oz." Sunny raised the limp cat in her arms.

"How about…Toto?"

"Nope." Sunny grinned, clearly enjoying the guessing game.

The cat was Oz.... "Is it Wizard?"

"That's it!"

Sunny's delight had Mariah smiling, feeling as if she'd suddenly been swept over a rainbow herself, onto this picturesque miniature farm. If it had started snowing on poppies, she wouldn't have been surprised. Rafe regarded her with a reluctant grin that only added to her enchantment.

Sobering, she reminded herself that any warming she sensed here was only because she'd declined to write the feature on Rafe. And she realized bleakly that she'd thrown away her chance to keep a job she couldn't afford to lose, all because of the dangers of a storm.

But as she stood in this over-the-rainbow setting, with its Ozlike characters and Rafe's ever-changing gaze heating her through, she knew it was he who posed the greatest threat to her well-being. It was a good thing she would be going home tomorrow, putting the crazy storm chaser behind her.

But escape didn't seem quite so imminent when Sunny said with her quiet intensity, "Dad, I want Mariah to write about you."

Chapter Four

A quiet fell, not unlike the calm before the storm, Mariah thought, uneasy.

Sunny's wish for her to write a feature on her father had Dorothy resting her hand on the girl's shoulder, while Rafe's stony silence spoke volumes. Photographing a tornado had apparently won her Sunny's trust in a way she'd failed to win Rafe and Dorothy's. The sky seemed to darken along with Rafe's mood, evening shadows etching the rustic landscape of his home and the handsome lines of his face. Mariah found herself uncharacteristically searching for words. "I'm... flattered, Sunny, but as I said, someone else would be better suited to write your dad's story."

Sunny hugged her cat tighter, Oz twitching his tail, both the girl and her cat condemning her with their stares. "But you got a picture of the tornado."

"That was just a matter of luck."

"And you helped my dad so he could drive out of the storm. You weren't even afraid of the hail."

Oh, yes, I was. If anything, Rafe's countenance grew more grim. She didn't want to say anything that would upset the girl, but neither could she contribute to Sunny's misconception. Besides being harmful to Sunny, a lie could come back to haunt her should another storm roll through before morning. Today had given her a whole new perspective on the weather. She wouldn't need her mother phoning to remind her to go to the basement the next time a tornado warning was issued.

"I'd say Mariah has a healthy respect for storms. And I'd say there's been enough written about Stormy Taylor." Rafe came to the rescue— though he obviously saw it as rescuing his daughter from *her.*

"But, Dad, you said those other journalists told lies. Mariah's *nice.* She won't tell lies, will you, Mariah?"

Rafe's impatient shift conveyed his doubt clearly.

Mariah raised her chin. "No, I would not tell lies. But—"

"You would write about Wizard, wouldn't you?"

"Well, of course, if that was what you wanted—"

"I do!" Sunny plopped Oz on the ground, the cat pinning its ears, indignant. "No one else wrote about my new pony."

Somehow, Mariah doubted that. The research she'd procrastinated over would probably reveal that plenty of ruthless journalists had exploited the fact that Rafe bought his grieving child a pony. She could easily imagine the press he'd shielded Sunny from, judging by the suspicion burning in his eyes. She felt a tug of compassion, aware Rafe only wanted to protect his daughter. "Thank you, Sunny, for believing I'm an honest journalist. However—"

Rafe muttered beneath his breath. *Oxymoron?* Was *that* what he'd said?

Mariah clenched her jaw. On the other hand, it was insulting to have her integrity doubted by a thrill chaser like "Stormy" Taylor.

"Dad, *please,* let her stay."

Her heart squeezed with Sunny's heartfelt plea. As Rafe drew his daughter aside, she resisted the urge to comfort the little girl. Sunny wasn't her child. Anything she might say would only invite further disparagement from Rafe.

A tear glistened on Sunny's cheek. Mariah felt a pang, knowing Sunny would soon be a disappointed little girl. As for herself, she knew nature had made a grave mistake, to have her be kissed by tornado-chasing Rafe on the same day her longing for a child revealed itself. The yearning she felt as he brushed away Sunny's tear made her grateful he was as determined as she to have her on her way back to Wichita.

Only Rafe's resolve seemed to melt away with the touch of a single tear. "All right," he growled. "Mariah can stay. She can write the feature."

No, I can't!

Sunny wrapped her arms around her father. "Thank you, thank you, thank you!"

Mariah exchanged glares with Rafe overtop of Sunny's head, only to glance away, unnerved by the heated undercurrent.

Dorothy, though clearly taken aback by Rafe's turnabout, covered it with smooth politeness. "Sunny, why don't you show Mariah your pony while I see to the food."

And have a talk with your father. It went without saying. Well, Mariah planned on having a chat with Rafe, too. Something along the line of reminding him she'd decided *not* to write the feature. He had a lot of nerve, ignoring her decision.

"Wizard loves company in the barn at night." Sunny beamed, too pleased to sense the brewing tension. "Come on."

"I'll tag along." Rafe started off with his daughter, no doubt loathe to leave Sunny alone with her. One more insult to her integrity. Thanking Dorothy for her hospitality, she stalked after Rafe. Sunny skipped alongside him, Oz loping ahead. Mariah pressed her lips as she caught up to them. Nothing she had to say to Rafe was fit for Sunny's ears.

But her pique gave way to wonder as they neared the barn. Was it only hours ago she'd almost been zapped by lightning, seeking out horses on the other side of a wire fence? In contrast to that stormy scene, the cozy little barn ahead seemed straight out of the Land of Oz, colorful even in the waning light, yellow sunflowers sprouting against its backdrop of red paint. She wouldn't be surprised to find a many-colored horse inside, just like in the movie.

Indeed, the pony who peered at them through his stall gate was colorful, his coat marked in large splotches of glossy chocolate and white, frosty streaks in his wavy mane and tail. Oz curled up on a bale of hay, while Sunny swung open the top half of the gate. Wizard shuffled over, blinking lazily in the glare of the fluorescent light Rafe switched on.

"Isn't he *beautiful?*" Sunny sighed the words, a girl in love with her horse. Mariah gazed at the stodgy pony, with its fuzzy foretop and sleepy eyes, thinking cuddly was a more apt description. But then, that was the wonder of being a child, viewing the world from the other side of the rainbow, instead of the stark black and white of reality.

"Dad got him for me last fall," Sunny went on. "He's really smart. That's why I named him Wizard."

Wizard and Oz. Mariah smiled at the spotted pony, gold cat and young girl with the Dorothy braids, a little caught up in the magic herself. It was easy to forget that not even ruby slippers could give Sunny the one thing she likely wished for—to have her mother back.

"*The Wizard of Oz* is our favorite movie," Sunny informed her.

Rafe wouldn't appreciate word of that getting around, tarnishing his daredevil image. But he seemed to have forgotten there was a journalist present, sharing an unguarded smile with his daughter that somehow weakened Mariah's knees even as it made her throat go tight.

"Dad watched it every year, growing up. So

that's what we did, too. Me and Dad and Mom. Grandma watched it with us this year.'' Sunny grew absorbed in straightening her pony's foretop, while Rafe turned somber, an exquisite pain coming into his eyes. Sunny wasn't the only one who could be hurt if forced to relive the memory of Ann's death.

Wizard bobbed his head, mussing his foretop, bringing back Sunny's laughter. And just as the magic rolled over Mariah again, she realized how rigidly Rafe stood, his grief hidden by simmering mistrust. A pall settled over her, as if the Wicked Witch of the West had dropped out of the sky. Recalling how the fictional Dorothy had melted the Wicked Witch by throwing a pail of water on her, she eyed the pony's water bucket, locked in the stall.

Never a pail of water handy when you needed one.

"Why don't you give Grandma a hand at the house. I need to talk to Mariah a moment."

"About Wizard? I can tell her about Wizard. And Oz, too. Oz would like to be in the story—"

"It isn't a story, it's *real,*" Rafe corrected sharply. Mariah pressed her lips. What a trial it must be, harboring all that animosity. Sunny quieted, and she tried not to be moved by the regret that softened Rafe's gaze. "It's been a long day. I think both Grandma and Mariah would appreciate your help.''

''Okay.'' Sunny hugged her pony, then moved toward the door. Just as Mariah thought the child would leave her father to suffer in her silent wake, she spun back, brightening. ''Mariah can bunk with me! You can have the bottom bunk, so you won't fall,'' she added solicitously.

After almost being carried off by a tornado, a fall from a bunk bed sounded trivial. ''I'd love—''

''Let's give Mariah time to think it over.''

''Oh, Daddy. She *wants* to.''

''Sunny…''

''I'm going.'' Rolling her eyes with theatric drama, Sunny exited the barn. They watched until she was silhouetted in the glow of the porch lamp Dorothy had turned on. Once the front door closed behind her, Mariah faced Rafe squarely. He wanted to talk? Well, so did she.

But the quiet of the small barn seemed to crowd her senses with the sweetness of hay and grain, the lingering warmth of the day wrapping Rafe's presence around her. Once again, words failed her.

Not so for Rafe.

''Sunny can be outspoken when the mood strikes. I won't have you taking advantage of that while you're here.''

''You seem to have forgotten—I'm not writing

the feature. Now how am I supposed to explain to Sunny that I won't be staying?''

"You can't, no more than I could."

His simplistic rationale infuriated her, in part because there was truth to it; she couldn't envision herself telling Sunny, *Sorry, but I won't be writing about you and your cat and your pony.*

"You did say you wanted to save your job."

Not at the expense of my life.

Still, Rafe's prodding reminded her of why she'd sought him out in the first place. She'd worked hard to gain the financial security that came with writing for the magazine. Maybe raising a child was what she wanted, but that didn't change the fact that she needed to earn a living. Bleak reality washed over her. She had no desire to spend the next two weeks chasing tornadoes. Especially now that she knew the tornado could wind up chasing her. *Especially now that Rafe had kissed her.*

Mariah plucked a straw from the pony's mane, bending the fragrant stem with her fingers. She'd once read how a tornado had embedded a straw stem in a tree trunk—definitely a force to be reckoned with. She hadn't felt much more substantial than this broken stem when she'd watched the tornado close in. She shivered, reliving their escape with the clarity of a nightmare.

"What happened today—the tornado—you won't have to take that risk again." Rafe stepped close to her as he spoke, reading her fear as only a fearless storm chaser could. Mariah sank against the stall boards, hugging her arms across her middle. His words made her feel safe, while his nearness left her uncertain. That same tingly feeling she'd had standing near the fence before the lightning strike prickled through her.

"You don't have to go on the road with me—I can report what happens. And you won't need to delve into our private lives. Just mention Wizard and Oz, and Sunny will be happy."

Mariah met Rafe's gaze with dawning awareness. Sunny wasn't the only one who would be happy if that was all she wrote. What he suggested was that she write a piece of fluff—as if her work was inconsequential.

Which was pretty much the approach *she'd* taken these past few months....

He *knew* she was afraid. And to protect his family, he would willingly exploit her newfound fear of tornadoes if she stayed. Judging by her reaction to him in this cozy setting, he could exploit more than just her fear if she didn't take charge of the situation.

Uncertainty fled. Mariah straightened, anger diffusing any sparks between them. "It isn't my way to sit back and let someone dictate what I write. Either I go on the road and gather the information I deem necessary, or there is no feature."

"All right." He set his jaw stubbornly. "But I don't want you questioning my daughter. I don't want her upset."

Only the remnants of pain in his eyes kept her voice even. "Believe it or not, I don't pry information from children."

Mariah pushed past him, marching out of the barn. She stopped just outside, struck by the realization that she'd played right into his reluctant hand. She was going to stay. She was going to write the feature.

Behind her, the barn went dark, the square of light at her feet disappearing. Rafe strode up beside her and they struck out for the house in silence, the porch lamp glowing in ironic welcome.

Crossing the yard, she eyed the sturdy planked door of the storm cellar. She'd seen that movie where the twister sucked up the cellar door and the man inside, trying to hold it closed. That could have been her today, sucked up by the tornado they'd narrowly eluded. Staying in the company of "Stormy" Taylor only promised more of the same.

Just as troubling was the animosity she would have to deal with. She wasn't used to all this resentment. *Plain View* was a quality magazine meant to acquaint readers with the plains. Most folks were honored to be selected for an interview.

Climbing the porch steps, she realized she'd forgotten her purse and equipment in Rafe's truck. Her lack of food and sleep hit her with all the might of a storm. Almost getting swept away must have this exhaustive effect on a person.

Rafe held open the door. "I'll bring in your things after we eat."

Her weariness must have shown. She passed by him, feeling his warmth, breathing his scent, aware the attraction between them posed the greatest problem of all.

They went straight to the kitchen, where the odd juxtapose of antiques and technology somehow managed to convey the homey ambiance she'd felt outside. Scanners and radios sat on a doily-covered chest. On the countertop, below oak cupboards, a small TV was tuned in low to The Weather Channel. But it was the spaghetti and salad Dorothy had lain out on the table that won Mariah's attention. Dorothy left them to eat, checking on Sunny, who was upstairs having a bath.

Mariah was halfway through her plate of spaghetti when the radio crackled.

Rafe rose to accept the transmission from his partner.

"Go ahead, Jeremy."

"Still got that journalist hounding you, or did the tornado scare her off?"

Mariah pressed her lips as Rafe curved his wryly. "That's a 10-12, pal." Lowering the mike, he explained briefly, "Visitor's present."

Had he just shared a joke with her? The grin Rafe flashed was likely for his own benefit, but Mariah felt her heart drumming anyway.

There was a moment of dead air before Jeremy responded, "My apologies, Miss Morgan." Then he added, "Does this mean I won't get a mention in the feature?"

Mariah rolled her eyes while Rafe muttered something about a comic book. That the men were friends as well as chase partners was obvious. Given the risks they took, trying to outwit the elements for a chance at a photograph, she wondered how Ann Taylor had coped. If she'd read the atmosphere at the café right, Trixie already recognized the wisdom of keeping the charming Jeremy at arm's length. As for herself, she was far too fascinated with storm-chasing Rafe.

"Pick up any souvenirs today?" Jeremy transmitted.

"Hail damage," Rafe replied. "I'll run the truck in for repairs first thing in the morning. But tell Trixie we'll be back to pick up Mariah's car tomorrow."

"Roger that. I'm heading down into Oklahoma now."

"Keep an eye on the sky. We've got a lot of moisture working up from the Gulf, and the way the jet stream's moving…"

Rafe hesitated, aware Mariah listened. The curious light in her eyes told him she'd be asking questions as soon as he signed off. "We ought to see some storm development in the next couple days."

"10-4. Say goodnight to the ladies for me."

Rafe signed off.

"So, you track the weather, like a meteorologist?" At his nod, she went on, "And you've determined another tornado is likely?"

"With the right dynamics to lift the air…the key elements are there." He cut short his explanation on the development of a storm. She was probably just leery of another close call like she'd had today. Or maybe, like so many others before her, she was working her way around to asking about the night Ann was killed. "You ask a lot of questions."

She raised her chin, reading him clearly. "As I told you, the focus of my work is to raise awareness of the danger of storms and the tornadoes they produce."

"Maybe that's your intention, but I've been

burned by 'well-meaning' journalists before. And it's hard to tell how low a person will go when her job is on the line.''

Bare feet smacked the hardwood floor of the hall in quick, small steps. Mariah's grimace transformed, her expression softening when Sunny bounded across the kitchen dressed in blue pajamas with fluffy white clouds on them. As Sunny wrapped her arms around him, he could almost mistake the emotion in Mariah's eyes for longing. But then, he had something she wanted; the story that would save her job.

''Grandma has some clothes upstairs for Mariah to wear after she showers,'' Sunny announced. ''I picked out one of your new T-shirts for her to sleep in, Dad. The green one.''

It would reach to Mariah's knees, like a night-gown. He imagined her lying in bed—*his* bed—wearing nothing more than his T-shirt. Mariah looked as unnerved as he felt. As if she might have similar thoughts.

''Come on, Mariah.'' Sunny tugged her along, the novelty of sharing bunk beds with Mariah enough to send her voluntarily to bed. He trusted his mother would put an end to that notion, trusted Mariah had picked up on his disapproval of the idea earlier. Still, he made a point of reminding Sunny, ''I'll be up to tuck you in.''

He frowned after them, their hands clasped as they left the room beaming smiles at each other. Unsettled, he went outside, checking on the pony one last time before gathering Mariah's equipment from his battered truck. As he turned toward the house, the upstairs lights went off, except for the one in Sunny's room, dimly lit by the night-light she sometimes left on since her mother's death.

He carted the laptop, recorder, cell phone and Mariah's purse inside. He hauled them up to the guest room, finding only her blue suit folded on the bed, her tattered hose in a crumpled mound atop it. Stowing her gear on the bed, he moved down the hall to his daughter's room. He peeked in the door. Sunny shot up in the upper bunk, touching her finger to her lips, then pointing to the bunk below.

Mariah lay on her stomach, facing the wall, her hand curled upon one of Sunny's lavender pillow cases. Her hair shone damply in the dim glow of light, curling past her shoulders, longer than he'd imagined....

"She's sleeping, Dad."

In my green T-shirt. And I'm the last person you have to worry will wake her up.

"Grandma said Mariah hasn't been sleeping well. She can tell by her eyes."

All he knew was that Mariah's eyes were very

blue and innocent and determined. A dangerous mix. But his mother was right, she was tired, falling asleep each time they hit the road. He only hoped she'd been too tired to interrogate his daughter, as his mother apparently assumed.

"Mariah tucked me in already."

It should have been Ann tucking her in. The painful knowledge that he couldn't fix his little girl's hurt mixed with the guilty awareness that Ann wouldn't have been here to tuck Sunny in even if there had been no storm, no accident.

"I said my prayers. Mariah listened."

Mariah listened to her prayers....

In that moment it struck him just what Sunny's prayers might entail, that his daughter might believe the answer to her prayers slept in the bunk below her.

"Daddy? Aren't you going to tuck me in, too?"

He crossed the room, though it cost him, his heart and mind in a turmoil. The lavender sheet flowed over Mariah's body, revealing her curves. The room seemed warm, but Sunny didn't object as he pulled her sheet up to her chin. She lay back, framed by lavender ruffles, looking all too pleased as she said, "Mariah's different than the other journalists, isn't she?"

She was different, all right. He hadn't wanted to kiss any of the other journalists prying into his life.

And his daughter hadn't wanted to have a slumber party with them.

Apparently, Sunny's was a statement of fact, for she went on without need of the reply he struggled for. "Can I go with you to get Mariah's car? *Please?* Grandma said we can use her truck."

"We'll see." How had he not seen this coming? He'd assumed Sunny was impressed over Mariah photographing a tornado. Now he felt a touch of panic over the prospect of the three of them traveling down the road together, could sense trouble brewing like a storm on the horizon. Sunny would come to love Mariah, and then Mariah would leave....

But surely not in only two weeks' time. He wouldn't let that happen; Sunny had suffered enough hurt. He touched her hair, still in braids, so she wouldn't have to comb it in the morning. "Go to sleep now. I love you, Sunshine."

"Me and Mom. You loved her, too, didn't you?"

Relief swept over him. How could he have thought Sunny would want another mother—especially when she had her grandma to turn to. "I'll always love your mother, Sunny. She gave you to me."

"I love you, Daddy." The bed squeaked as she reached out, hugging him tightly.

In the bunk below, Mariah heard Rafe kiss his daughter, heard the sheet rustle as he tucked her in. He crossed the room with heavy steps, closing the door softly behind him.

I'll always love your mother....

Mariah spent another sleepless night, wondering if she might save her job at the expense of her heart.

Chapter Five

Rain.

Mariah vaguely recalled being worried about another storm. Another tornado. But the fresh smell of rain she breathed made her feel safe and warm. She burrowed deeper into her covers.

Blinking, Mariah came fully awake, her nose buried in the crook of her arm and the soft sleeve of Rafe's green T-shirt. She drew another breath. Indeed, his shirt had a clean-washed scent, fresh like the rain. Like Rafe…

Rolling onto her back, she gazed at the underside of Sunny's top bunk. This must be her writer's mind at work, creating a romantic image of a crazy storm chaser. Maybe she was writing for the wrong kind of publisher.

Though Rafe did carry the scent of rain....

From outside came the clang of a bucket, then a creak alternating with the gush of water. A well. Careful not to bump her head, she crawled from the low bunk, crossing the lavender-carpeted floor to the window. Pushing her tangled hair past her shoulder, she pressed her nose to the screen.

Oh, my.

Rafe manned the pump, his booted foot braced on the wooden boards that framed the well, his denim shirt sleeves skimming the swell of his sun-browned biceps. His tawny hair seemed to absorb and reflect the rays, strands falling over his forehead as he bent to his task. Water splashed, drops transformed into silver sparks in the morning light. Sunflowers turned their bright faces to the dawn, while Wizard thrust his pretty head out the barn window to neigh "good morning."

She was still in Oz....

Rafe raised his head, his gaze shooting to Sunny's window. Even from a distance, she sensed his scrutiny, making her conscious of her tangled hair, of his T-shirt resting precariously at the point of her shoulder. He slowly straightened, and she sensed his caution, too, laced with an awareness she shared, electrified tenfold by their single kiss. She ought to step away....

A rustling from the bed announced Sunny's

waking, the child pushing aside her ruffled sheets to clamber down the ladder from her bunk. She ran over to peer out the window, waving and calling to her father and pony. Rafe waved to his daughter, then hoisted the bucket from beneath the spigot, carrying it back to the barn.

Well. Mariah turned from the window and smiled down at Sunny, the little girl adorable in her cloud pajamas and mussed braids. "Good morning. Thank you for letting me bunk with you."

"You're welcome. Last night, Grandma said I should leave you alone in the morning so you can get dressed. And Dad said 'we'll see' if I can ride along to get your car. I'll go find out right now." Sunny spun for the door, a minitornado, calling back as she raced down the hall, "I'll tell Grandma you're awake."

If only *she* had that much enthusiasm over spending time in the company of Stormy Taylor. Mariah stepped over to the bed, flipping covers neatly over each bunk. Sooner or later, she'd wind up chasing another tornado, her life on the line again. She'd be lucky to survive, let alone write a feature or go on to raise the child she wanted.

But as she smoothed her hand over Sunny's lavender sheets, her gaze drifted to the window. Her heart drummed a telling beat. The truth was,

Rafe intrigued her in ways that had nothing to do with his career. Somehow, she had to remain focused on getting the story she needed to save her job. As loving as her home life had been, she had no desire to raise a child of her own in the level of poverty she'd grown up in.

Mariah gave the coverlet one last tug. Arranging a stuffed dog that looked amazingly like Toto upon Sunny's ruffled pillow, she couldn't help thinking how nice it would be, spending time in the company of the little girl—as long as she remembered she was in ''Oz,'' that the motherly feeling coming over her for Sunny wasn't real.

Back in the guest room, Mariah dug a hair band from her purse, gathering her unruly hair into a thick ponytail. It felt like old times, dressing in her borrowed clothes, the way she used to dress in her sister Madeline's hand-me-downs—something her child *wouldn't* have to do. Pulling on white socks, a green plaid shirt that fit snugly and was likely Dorothy's, and a pair of jeans that were comfortably too big to have belonged to Sunny's slim Grandma, she went down to the kitchen.

Sunny was working on a short stack of pancakes, Dorothy flipping more at the stove. Considering Sunny wasn't at the barn begging her father to take her to Trixie's, she assumed Grandma must have set Sunny's priorities straight.

Taking the stack of pancakes Dorothy offered with her "good morning," Mariah thanked her, adding, "I appreciate the clothes, too."

"They're clean, but nothing fancy—a mix of Rafe's and mine and those jeans, which were collected for the church rummage sale. I'm on the committee. I hope you don't mind second-hand, but you're a mite curvier than me. You can help yourself to slip-on canvas shoes donated new by the pharmacy. Make do, or do without, I guess."

Dorothy said it all with an "Auntie Em" practicality that reminded Mariah not only of Dorothy's aunt from *The Wizard of Oz,* but fondly of her mother. She eyed the box of shoes—red canvas slip-ons.

"Ruby slippers," Rafe murmured from outside the screened kitchen door. Then his gaze met hers and practicality fled, the heat in his eyes triggering a hot wash of desire.

Rafe stifled a groan and pushed open the door. He had to agree, his mother was right; the plaid shirt fit just snug enough to enhance Mariah's more generous curves. He'd barely gotten over the images burned into his mind of her standing at the window; her curling dark hair, her almost bare shoulder, *his* T-shirt.

Mariah straightened in her chair. "Those shoes

will be fine." She smoothed the hem of her shirt. "I grew up wearing my sister's hand-me-downs."

A weary acceptance crept into her voice that spoke of a long term relationship with wearing handed-down clothes. On the basis of her snazzy suit, he hadn't imagined her as a child who'd had to "make do." He realized she'd become a woman who didn't have to—as long as she kept her job at *Plain View Magazine.*

Mariah raised her chin knowingly, the air between them thickening as though the barometer had taken an ominous drop.

"Dad, can I go with you?"

"She hasn't seen Jess in a while," his mother pointed out from the stove, cutting off his instinctive refusal. For some reason, her resentment of journalists seemed to waiver with Mariah, for whom she obviously felt a measure of trust where Sunny was concerned. It must be a woman-to-woman thing, because he sure wasn't feeling it. He didn't trust *himself* when it came to Mariah.

Since Ann's death, his mother had been there for him with Sunny, helping them to get through one day at a time. This was one of those rare times she'd attempted to influence his decision where his daughter was concerned. That she had seemed reason enough to heed her input. Though Sunny awaited his answer far too intently, he pushed aside his misgivings and strolled over to give one of her braids a tug. "I guess you'd better come along then."

Sunny hopped up on her chair to hug him, then scrambled down before he had a chance to tell her to do so. "I have to get on my clothes!"

Trading grins with Mariah, she ran out of the room. Mariah's obvious affection for his daughter did nothing to quell Rafe's unease. But as the thunder of Sunny's small feet faded, leaving the room uncomfortably quiet, his unease gave way to that pulsing awareness of Mariah that clouded his judgment and promised turbulent times ahead. He could only hope his mother knew best, sending the three of them on the road together.

With Sunny to hurry them along, they were soon on their way. Mariah and Sunny followed him first to the service station, where he left his truck for repairs. He joined them in his mother's pickup, Sunny sitting between them on the functional bench seat, the sun in their eyes as they headed east along Highway 54. With Sunny narrating their journey out of town, Rafe thought wryly that he needn't have worried about Mariah questioning his daughter; she wouldn't have a chance to speak.

"A tornado hit Tassel a *long* time ago, when Dad was a kid, like me. Right, Dad?"

"Yeah. A *long* time ago," Rafe responded dryly, drawn to smile in answer to Mariah's grin.

"Lots of people he knew got hurt because they didn't know the tornado was coming. That's why he takes pictures of storms, to help scientists learn when a tornado will form. Then they can warn people faster, right, Dad?"

"Yeah." Though it seemed a long time ago, as well, that anyone other than family and peers recognized the focus of his work. The thrill of the chase had become the focus when it came to telling his story.

Although, he had to admit, Mariah hadn't seemed very "thrilled" yesterday. After their narrow escape from the tornado's path, she'd been ready to abandon her story. He'd been a fool to convince her to stay for Sunny's sake, knowing the feature was necessary to save her job. In his mind, that only made Mariah more desperate, and his daughter more vulnerable.

"I was at my Grandma's house when my mom left home before the warning siren went off."

Rafe glanced sharply at Sunny, his chest tight. Sometimes, like last night, the fact that Sunny missed her mother was painfully evident. Other times, like now, he had to remind himself she didn't know her mother had deserted them.

"She wouldn't have left if she'd heard the siren,'' Sunny added solemnly, squinting into the sun.

Guilt bore down on him, as did Mariah's assessing gaze, almost as if she could read the truth of Ann's leaving in his eyes. Surprisingly, she said nothing, giving Sunny's jeans-clad knee a squeeze. Then she proceeded to point out Sunny's favorite landmark. ''Isn't that the Lightning Tree I saw last night?''

Sunny launched into a monologue, but it wasn't long before she sagged against Mariah's shoulder, as if lulled to sleep by the sound of her own voice. He frowned as her small hand came to rest over Mariah's, still curled upon her knee, Mariah's crimson nails bright against Sunny's dark blue jeans.

''You can shift her my way. She won't wake up.''

''She's fine,'' Mariah said defensively, then resumed her gentle regard of his daughter. ''I'm sorry about her mother.''

And curious, he could tell, despite her caring tone. ''Ann left on a trip before the siren sounded.''

How was it he felt guilty, hedging the truth, when he was only protecting his child? ''I was out chasing storms when it happened.''

Rafe pushed his hand through his hair and focused on the road. He hadn't told her anything the whole world didn't already know, but her compassionate murmur made him regret the impulse. He suspected Mariah, with her concerned blue eyes, would be all too easy to confide in. He braced himself now for the personal questions that were sure to follow.

"Was that a motel?"

Not the question he expected, but it made him uneasy all the same. Her gaze narrowed as they passed by an unassuming building of nondescript landscaping, one of the few roadside motels they'd driven by last night. "How *nice* of you to let me sleep last night, rather than wake me to stay at a motel."

She obviously realized he hadn't wanted to wake her and deal with her questions or his attraction to her, any more than he had when they'd chased yesterday's storms. But the whole truth was, he hadn't been able to bring himself to leave her. He'd stayed in enough cheap motels to know the pitfalls—questionable privacy, no hot water, dubious bedding. He'd felt protective of her at the same time he'd been protecting himself *from* her. But he wasn't about to tell her that.

"No problem," he muttered, and concentrated on the road ahead as best he could with her glaring at him.

But Mariah's glare transformed into contemplation of Rafe as he drove, breeze through the window spiking his hair. His denim shirt was untucked
and unbuttoned, a clean white T-shirt showing beneath. His usual unfettered style, from what she
had seen. She'd also seen the pain in his eyes over
Ann; had sensed his guilt that he hadn't been there
to stop his wife from venturing out into the storms
he'd chased, ironically, with the purpose of pre-
venting tragedy. And yet…she sensed something
more, his manner turning evasive, almost as if he
had something to hide.

Sunny sighed against her, the child's warm
weight stirring her own protective instinct. The
longing she now recognized as a yearning for a
child unfurled achingly within her. If the storm
hadn't led to the revelation that she wanted a child,
Sunny's sweet adoration surely would have. Still,
she refrained from wrapping her arm about Sunny
as the little girl slept. Sunny had her Grandma to
fill the void in her life; she didn't need Mariah
confusing the issue.

They rode in silence. Mariah noticed another of
the sparsely scattered cottonwoods, its stark,
stripped branches similar to that of Sunny's Lightning Tree. She stared in passing, her thoughts bus-
ily shifting between her motherly and journalistic
instincts. She caught her lip, loathe to ask the myr-

iad questions forming in her mind, still stinging over the way Rafe had left her to sleep yesterday.

But Rafe apparently noted her interest in the tree and offered another of his reluctant explanations, likely driven by his daughter's desire for her to write the feature. "Most times, trees will survive a direct hit by lightning with little damage. The current passes over their surface to the ground."

Rafe warmed to his subject and she found his revelations on the weather more in-depth and fascinating than any of her high school science classes. By the time Sunny woke, they were almost to the café. Sunny radioed ahead to Jess, the children manning the CB with expert ease.

The sun was barely noon high when they pulled in at Trixie's. The trip had passed quickly. But as Mariah climbed from the truck, hot breeze stole her breath, and it suddenly seemed days since she'd abandoned her rental car here. She felt as if she'd experienced a time warp, as if she'd really been in "Oz." She recognized the battered truck Rafe's partner, Jeremy, had sped off in yesterday, and it wasn't long before they were gathered inside at the counter for lunch with Jeremy and Jess. Once the meager noon crowd left, Trixie joined them, leaning against the counter to chat.

Sunny and Jess soon abandoned their cheeseburgers to play the pinball machine, Jeremy raining quarters into their hands and ignoring Trixie's disapproving glare. He and Rafe excused themselves to check out the forecast on Jeremy's laptop at a nearby table, acting pretty much like the kids, Mariah thought wryly.

She took Trixie up on her offer of chocolate cake, the two of them smiling over the antics of Sunny and Jess in a manner that left Mariah wistful. But it wasn't long before the atmosphere over the laptop electrified, stormy weather apparently forecast somewhere. As Jeremy pushed his chair from the table, Mariah peered out the front window, uneasy, no longer making assumptions about sunny skies.

"Tornado watch around Amarillo. Looks to be busy in Texas these next few days." Jeremy shut down the laptop, eyeing his partner as Rafe kicked back in his chair. "Going to tag along?"

Sunny stopped watching Jess play pinball to ask in her serious manner, "Can I go, Dad?"

"Me, too," Jess piped up.

Surely not...

Rafe probably longed to give chase, as Jeremy obviously did, but it didn't show as he replied calmly, "You know better, Sunny. And I'm not chasing anything but Trixie's chocolate cake today."

No, dear, you can't chase tornadoes today. He sounded almost like a normal father, telling his child, no, you can't play in the street. He seemed content to spend a quiet day with his daughter. Sunny was the one who was disappointed, the way she'd been yesterday when she learned Rafe hadn't gotten a picture of the funnel. Despite that her mother had perished during a tornado, she seemed unafraid to face a storm in Rafe's presence, obviously viewing her storm-chasing father as invincible.

Sunny turned back to her game with Jess. Jeremy eyed the two sulking children, Trixie folding her arms and frowning as if to say, *See what you did?* Mariah hid a grin as Jeremy muttered a facetious goodbye to himself and strode out the door.

Rafe sauntered over, settling onto the stool beside her. Trixie served his cake, letting the plate drop with a rattle, her pique with Jeremy carrying over to his partner before she said grudgingly, "At least one of you has some sense today."

Trixie stalked off. Curious, Mariah swiveled her stool toward Rafe. Refraining from more personal questions, she asked, "Aren't you worried you'll miss the photo opportunity of a lifetime?"

Rafe faced her, his long legs framing hers. "Did you know that less than fifty percent of the approximately one thousand tornadoes officially recorded each year are chaseable? Fewer still can be photographed, occurring at night or without warning. They travel at speeds of forty to sixty miles per hour, lasting ten minutes on average; some only a moment. Humidity and dust often distort any images you get—that's if you manage to get close enough for a picture."

"And your point is?"

"I'm probably not missing anything, taking a day off during the chase season. I'm just trying to raise your awareness of the odds. You did say your feature was focused on the storms I photograph."

The challenge behind his words told her he saw past her simple question to the curiosity beneath. She was being judged unfairly by the actions of others, and his low regard of her as a journalist rankled. If anything, she'd shown great restraint in regard to his personal life. "My awareness was raised plenty yesterday, thank you."

Rafe grinned at that, and for a moment, she had no focus at all beyond his curving sexy mouth. Taking his plate of cake in hand, he rose to join the children at the pinball machine. She thought wryly that a photograph of him smiling would significantly enhance the human interest aspect of her feature, at least where female readers were concerned.

A moment later he was laughing with Sunny and

Jess while she mulled over the interesting information he'd parted with. Whenever he spoke of his work, he seemed to confirm her early impression that he wasn't crazy at all.

"You seem surprised." Trixie strolled over, pitcher in hand, and freshened Mariah's iced tea. "Rafe's driven, but he's not crazy like Jeremy. You shouldn't believe everything you read."

The fact was, Mariah thought guiltily, she hadn't read much. She hadn't done the extensive research she normally would have before attempting a feature. She hadn't even known Rafe lived on a magical farm, a "Land of Oz" he'd created just for his daughter.

"On the other hand, he *is* a storm chaser, and in his own way, just as driven as Jeremy." Trixie eyed her knowingly. "Jeremy says you stayed the night at Rafe's. It's not like him to take a journalist home."

"Sunny's the one who wanted me to stay," Mariah insisted, her face heating. But she sensed Rafe watching her, the way he had that morning, from a distance that failed to diminish their awareness of each other.

In his own way, Rafe's just as driven as Jeremy.

The sudden urge to know more about this man who chased storms and lived in "Oz" with his adorable daughter gripped her—her professional instincts finally kicking in. It was early enough in the day that she could drive to Wichita, do some research, then return to Rafe's place this evening.

Trixie got back to work, and Mariah slid off her stool, walking over to the pinball machine. Rafe straightened from where he leaned against it, coaching Jess and Sunny.

"I've decided to drive up to Wichita this afternoon to do some research in preparation for writing the feature."

Sunny stopped playing her game, abruptly halting the flashing lights and ringing bells. Standing on a chair as she was, there was no avoiding her stare. "Are you going to come back?"

Rafe seemed to await her answer as intently as Sunny, their duel gazes penetrating clear to her soul. Almost as if he wanted her to come back as much as Sunny wanted her to...

And for a moment, her desire to return had nothing to do with saving her job.

A whirl of emotion swept her, as unexpected as yesterday's tornado. *How had this happened so fast? How had she not seen this coming?*

Sunny had her Grandma, but that didn't mean the child wouldn't start to love her, only to be hurt when the time came for her to leave. As for Rafe— even if he did have feelings for her beyond the basic, which she doubted—he was the last kind of man she needed to fall for. There was no future for her in "Oz."

"Of course, I'll be back."

Mariah turned away, feeling their mistrustful gazes burning her back until she closed the door.

Daylight had faded to pink when Mariah emerged from the Wichita Public Library, copies of microfilm newsprint and magazine articles tucked beneath her arm, the rest of her research stored on a disk tucked in her purse. A frequent patron, she'd raised some brows with her borrowed clothes, "ruby slippers" and windblown ponytail, only then realizing she hadn't given a thought to her customary professional attire. The only evidence left of her professional image had been her expensive leather purse and crimson nails.

But that wasn't her concern as she settled herself in her rental coupe and made her way back to Highway 54. Somehow, despite all her research, she was left feeling there was something she'd missed, only adding to the sense Rafe had something to hide.

Her mind churned with the emerging pattern she'd seen in Rafe's life. His marriage to a lifelong sweetheart at the height of his notoriety, the decline of press-worthy chases after the birth of his child, the reemergence of his risk-taking in the aftermath of Ann's death. Almost as if he'd settled down when Sunny came along, only to revert to outlaw chases after his wife died. Driven in his own way, as Trixie had said, but just when Sunny needed him most...

The Yellow Brick Road unfurled before her, dusk giving way to stars by the time she rolled through Tassel, the town illuminated by a handful of streetlamps and the yellow squares of shade-drawn windows. She turned down the Taylors' lane, and the glow of the porch lamp lit the uncertain places in her heart, revealing Rafe propped against the porch rail, as if waiting for her.

Home. Family. Her heart's desire.

Mariah was tempted to click the heels of her ruby slippers. But she knew better. Knew she mustn't use Sunny to fulfill her longing for a child when Rafe was the wrong kind of man to love. He reminded her of Scarecrow from *The Wizard of Oz*; if he only had a brain. Then he'd realize how much his daughter needed him. Needed him not to take such risks...

Rafe straightened as Mariah emerged from the shadows of the yard into the soft cascade of light, suitcase in hand. Her exhaustion was evident in her heavy step, but he had too much emotion built up inside him to let things keep until morning. His daughter had waited for her on the porch until well after bedtime, then tossed and turned herself to sleep. Without preamble he told her, "Sunny was afraid you wouldn't come back."

Mariah glanced uncertainly at the darkened windows of the house as she climbed the steps. "Should I wake her?"

"She'd only have trouble getting back to sleep again." The guilt that darkened her eyes only managed to make him feel guilty, as well. Rafe sighed. "Go on to bed. Mom's got the guest room ready for you."

Mariah crossed to the door. "I'm sorry I worried Sunny."

"She'll get over it." *First thing tomorrow, when she sees you've come back.*

"Good night then."

The door closed behind her, and he was left alone with nothing but the truth to contend with.

And the truth was, he'd been afraid, too. His daughter wasn't the only one he was trying to protect.

Chapter Six

Time to hit the road again.

Rafe scanned the forecast and meteorological data on the computer monitor, but there was no hint of storm development anywhere close. Even Jeremy's Texas tornadoes had failed to pan out; the front had stalled to the west. Still, the panhandle was his best target area; he *had* to get back on the road. The trip to Trixie's yesterday had done nothing to discourage his daughter's growing infatuation with Mariah—not to mention his own. Chasing storms with Mariah wasn't likely to reverse the trend.

"Dad!"

Sunny thundered down the hall, her steps accompanied by a gentler footfall he already recognized as Mariah's. Resigned to the fact that she would be cuffed by his daughter's small hand, he rolled his oak chair from the desk to face them.

They halted in the doorway to the den. Sunny had dressed in jeans and her favorite lavender T-shirt, her hair neatly braided—by his mother or Mariah? he wondered testily. Mariah's curls tumbled past her shoulders in shining waves. Her lips were glossy rose, her eyes full of question as she checked out the computer screen.

Her curiosity reminded him of her reason for being here. He noticed it hadn't taken her long to shed her hand-me-downs for something more suitable—and expensive—in her role as journalist. She looked like a page out of L.L. Bean in her olive shorts and leather hiking boots. She wore her matching shirt like a jacket, and the ivory tank she had on beneath it had the shimmer of real silk.

Sunny beamed at Mariah, their hands entwined just as he'd known they would be. Rafe turned back briefly to shut down the computer. They could be in Amarillo in less than three hours.

"Dad, did you send in the film of Mariah's tornado to be processed yet?"

Mariah's tornado. Mariah smiled—a bit smugly, it seemed—and it grated on him that she'd gotten the shot he missed when he'd abandoned the shoot to get *her* to safety. Aware Sunny waited, he answered, "First thing this morning."

He always had his film developed as soon as possible. It was the only way to ensure exposed film was safe from damage. Still, he knew Sunny would be disappointed as he told her, "But we'll be a while getting the photos. The agency has a backlog of work."

Sunny frowned at that. Mariah did, too. Threatening twin vortices, he thought, trying not to grin as he pushed out of his chair and crossed the room. Tugging Sunny's braid, he assured them, "I explained we needed the photos as soon as possible."

That erased their frowns, but Rafe felt a frown of his own coming on with the knowledge that Mariah might want to use the photo in her feature. If it wasn't for Sunny's need of the picture, he'd be wishing Mariah had stuck her thumb over the lens. Changing the subject, he told them, "I need to join Jeremy in Amarillo today. Storms are brewing out west."

Mariah caught her lip, her apprehension over the prospect of chasing down another tornado evident. Still, she said determinedly, "I'm ready when you are."

She looked ready, all right, with her curls and silk. She raised storm-chasing fashion to a new level. In his faded khaki pants and black T-shirt, he felt underdressed.

He sidestepped around them, muttering, "I have to get my truck from the service station."

Mariah ended up driving him to the east edge of town, his mother in the midst of baking. Sunny tagged along, inspecting the live bait while he paid for the new windshield.

"Only got one left, Stormy," the mechanic informed him, and Mariah raised her brows.

"He keeps windshields in stock for you? This must play havoc with your insurance rates," she noted while the mechanic wrote up the ticket.

Rafe checked and found Sunny leaning over the live well. Assured she was totally absorbed with the minnows, he explained, "Hail damage is a common hazard during chase season. Then there are the occasional tree limbs and other flying objects—"

"I get the picture."

And he could see by her wary gaze that she did, her mind likely replaying their narrow escape from the storm. He reminded himself that he wanted her here to write the feature that would make his daughter happy. She couldn't do that if he scared her off.

"The storms are stalled west of the panhandle.

We'll wait them out or find another storm to chase. We won't get caught by surprise this time.''

''Okay.'' Mariah gave a nod of conviction.

''I'll gas up the truck, then we'll grab a change of clothes and hit the road.''

''*One* change of clothes?''

The tornado hadn't scared her off, but he should have known a lack of silk shirts would. ''All right, two. But that's it. I'm not leaving behind a single film pack just to make room for clothes.''

Rafe snatched the receipt the mechanic handed him and strode over to Sunny and her worms. A sight that reassured him his tomboy daughter and this woman were worlds apart. Then he noticed the fingers Sunny dipped in the minnow tank sported bright crimson nails.

''Dorothy said it was okay,'' Mariah said softly at his side. She grinned as Sunny closed her hand around a minnow.

It isn't okay, he wanted to say. He didn't share his mother's trust in this woman. But Sunny was grinning, too, so he only said, ''Let's go before we end up paying Mike for worn-out minnows.''

Back home, Dorothy put Sunny to work kneading dough. They were making plans for an afternoon ride on Wizard when Rafe and Mariah left, his resolve to capture a tornado on film for Sunny the driving force within him. As he pulled onto the highway, he could still feel the warmth of Sunny's arms wrapped around his neck for a hug.

Then Mariah brushed her hand along his jaw and he felt hot all over.

"You have flour on your face." She brushed at his cheek, down his neck, across his shoulder.... Apparently noticing his clenched jaw and stiff shoulders, she curled her pretty fingers and drew back her hand.

Miles passed before he could draw an even breath. By the time they'd networked the highways down into Oklahoma, heading west to the Texas panhandle, he'd decided that between her questions and her clingy silk top and her long smooth legs she was more distracting than any tornado had ever been. He found himself giving her the in-depth explanation on the development of storms he'd cut short her first night, and pointing out signs of previous storm damage. She learned to man the CB and use the handheld radio scanner to activate National Weather Service broadcasts. She seemed genuinely interested in his work, dogging his steps when he stopped to take photographs. It took effort to keep up his guard when she turned the conversation to his personal life, especially in the confines of the truck, when he couldn't hide behind his camera.

"You spend a lot of time on the road. Away

from family. I realize you would never put Sunny in danger, but I can't help but wonder if..."

Her voice trailed off. She wasn't as blunt as most, reminding him of her initial reluctance to write the feature. "Ann came along sometimes, to help when the press was involved."

Rafe caught himself before he revealed the *only* time Ann troubled herself with his work was when the press was involved. Mariah seemed to read his grim change in mood, quieting, aware the door had closed on the subject.

A few miles outside Amarillo, he got Jeremy on the CB and arranged to meet him at the National Weather Service office there.

Mariah perked up at the prospect. Observing tornadoes from the safety of the Amarillo office sounded much better than chasing them on the road.

Once there, Jeremy greeted them heartily. There was also a chase team of two cocky young men garbed in black leather, whom she assumed belonged to the turbo-charged black SUV parked outside. "Outlaws," Jeremy confided with a disparagement she was sure Trixie would find ironic. But when one of them took a shine to her, trying to impress her with a story of his latest narrow escape, it was Rafe who drew her away, wrapping his arm around her shoulder in a surprisingly protective manner.

"How am I supposed to work and babysit you at the same time?" he grumbled, once he'd pulled her aside.

So much for protective. He was annoyed with her. She was rather annoyed herself. "I can take care of myself, thank you." She sniffed in disdain at the outlaw chaser as he and his partner were discreetly ushered out the door. "His idea of a narrow escape pales in comparison to what I lived through the other day."

"You're a pro, all right," Rafe drawled dryly. Before she could bristle, he went on, "Come on. I'll introduce you to the Doppler radar system."

She was impressed with the Doppler radar, its data available via cellular phones and computers. Mostly she was impressed with Rafe. There was something incredibly sexy in the serious manner that came over him when he indulged her questions regarding his photography and the weather. On the road today, she'd become absorbed with his work, with *Rafe*. But when she'd steered the conversation toward the more personal aspects of his life, the sense of camaraderie had been broken, leaving her frustrated. Regretful…

She knew she should delve deeper, get to the root of his evasiveness. But the pain that came into his eyes when he talked of Ann always stopped her.

But a journalist couldn't afford to be sensitive to the point of jeopardizing her work. When Rafe settled into a seat in the office library and set to work on a forecast sheet, Mariah scooted her chair close, determined to stay on top of things. When she brushed against Rafe's muscled arm, she edged back again. She couldn't afford to be distracted, either.

Rafe charmed her anyway, reminding her endearingly of Sunny coloring with crayons as he used green, purple, red and blue markers to denote winds, moisture, pressures and temperatures. The maze of twisting lines and numbers only confused her. She couldn't help thinking his precision forecasting and chase preparation weren't in keeping with his outlaw image. Rafe read the forecast clearly, his disappointment evident. The front would remain stalled to the west today.

"Think I'll head back to Oklahoma," Jeremy said. "I could use a down day at the farm—roof leaks like a sieve."

Mariah suspected it wasn't a leaky roof that drew Jeremy back to Oklahoma, but rather Trixie. She traded knowing grins with Rafe, and the effusive warmth she felt had nothing to do with his chase partner's love life. So much for professionalism. She felt acutely conscious of the hours ahead, hours they would likely spend at some motel....

"We'll drive north," Rafe announced, effectively banishing any notion she had of observing storms by satellite. "If the front fizzles out, at least we'll be closer to home."

"You can always hope for a little West Texas magic," Jeremy said with a grin, giving them a wave on his way out.

"West Texas magic? What's that?" Mariah asked. It sounded almost...romantic.

"A severe storm that develops in the panhandle without warning," Rafe said dispassionately, and Mariah thought again that she might be in the wrong line of work where her imagination was concerned.

But there was no time to dwell on the notion. Rafe was ready to take to the highways again.

Once in the truck, Mariah stripped down to her silk tank top in deference to the late-day heat. She gathered her hair into a thick ponytail, securing it with a band from her purse. As she relaxed into the seat, she noticed Rafe had tensed up, probably due to the stalled storm front. He didn't seem inclined to talk as he backtracked on Highway 60, then turned north on 207, so she studied the Texas map as they drove. Since being pursued by a tornado, there was no underestimating the convenience of a handy side road.

After a while, she gazed out the window, lulled by the endless flow of fields. It was hard to imagine a tornado churning up the tranquil landscape, playing a game of hit and miss with the scattering of farmhouses in the peaceful setting....

She must have dozed. She opened her eyes as the truck bounced over ruts, Rafe pulling to the shoulder along a roadside ice cream stand that seemed to have been dropped in the middle of nowhere. She eyed the ramshackle row of motel rooms beyond it. The Cactus Motel. *Surely not...*

She climbed out and caught herself raising her face to the elements, the same as Rafe. The breeze was soft, the sun low and haloed. Wispy clouds had earlier streaked the sky; now white puffs dotted the waning blue like cottonballs. Pretty, she thought, if you didn't dwell on the motel.

"Warm front approaching. They move in slow, move on slow."

He was watching her now; she could feel his gaze, the way she felt the rays of the sun, warm and deep.

"We'll stay here tonight, get an early fix on the weather tomorrow."

Stay *here?* Now there was a thought to chill the heat inside her. "We don't have to stay *here.* I have an expense account. We can find something nicer.''

"I have an expense account, too," Rafe said. He seemed amused. "The next motel is forty miles away. I told Sunny I'd be settled in by eight. I always leave her a message, then she calls me once she's in bed.''

He called his daughter at night to "tuck her in." Another blow to his crazy storm chaser image.

"Be right back." He strode off, pulling open the creaky door to the motel office, not so much as a No Vacancy sign to turn him away.

Resigned to her fate, Mariah tried to look on the bright side, the way her mother had taught her to do. But it was impossible to find anything bright in the drab row of low-slung rooms that comprised The Cactus Motel.

Even Rafe seemed grim when he came back with the key. The *key*. Not keys.

"There's a baseball team booked here tonight. We have to share a room. And before you insist we drive on, I already called ahead. The next motel is full up, too—rodeo cowboys."

"But...but—"

"Competing for rooms this time of year is a hazard of chasing." No longer amused, he looked tired and stubborn. The shadow of beard on his jaw, which had been clean-shaven this morning, only added to the effect as he reminded her, "It was your choice to come along."

Mariah planted her hands on her hips as he dragged their meager bags from the truck. So much for the benefits of an expense account. So much for lounging around a motel pool, going over the day's notes. She marched after him to their room. He turned the key in the lock. The door swung open and stuck against the dirt-colored carpet.

Mariah peered inside. So much for privacy. The twin beds might as well have been a single, they were crowded so close together. What if Rafe snored? Even if he didn't, she'd be able to hear him breathe while he slept. And what about pajamas? She'd smuggled a pair along, but somehow, she doubted he had.

Sunny's bunk beds would have served them well now. Then she wouldn't be able to see him. Or catch the rain scent of him...

Mariah clenched her fists. Even in this, the most unromantic of motels, the chemistry between them thrived.

Rafe nudged her inside, taking three steps to the bed, dropping their bags on the mattresses. No bounce. They just settled into the sag. She liked a firm mattress. She liked fresh sheets and a hot bath in a clean tub. It didn't look like she would have either here.

Rafe telephoned home, leaving his message for Sunny. Trying to ignore his soft, affectionate tone, Mariah stepped over to the bed that would be hers, sinking onto the mattress. She pushed to her feet when she noticed Rafe flipping back the spread on his bed. He appeared to be checking for...it didn't bear thinking about. She did the same, peering cautiously between the sheets.

Rafe switched on the TV. Light flickered on the close beige walls and drapes. He seemed to accept the snowy picture as a matter of course as he tuned in—naturally—to a twenty-four-hour weather station. They stood staring at the blurred screen, their scents mingling, their breathing in sync, until the small room seemed to shrink to claustrophobic dimensions.

"I could use a cheeseburger," Rafe said, exhaling deeply.

For once, she was in perfect agreement.

They walked to the nearby ice cream stand, and dusted off a rusted, wrought iron table, seeking shade beneath the dubious protection of a faded blue umbrella to watch the sun go down. A truck rolled by on the highway, kicking up whirls of debris. Dust devils, Rafe called them. Minitornadoes, she thought wryly, covering her sandwich and milkshake, waiting for the grit to settle—on her.

And no decent bath awaiting. "How do you live like this?"

"Part of the job."

And he loved his work as a storm photographer. Given the circumstances, she could only view this as a timely reminder that he was not marriage material.

"You like being a journalist, don't you?"

What she didn't like was the straightforward way *he* had of questioning *her*, making her feel as if she was the one being interviewed. Self-conscious, as only Rafe could make her feel, she brushed dust from her silk shirt. "A successful career has always been important to me. Mom and Dad encouraged us kids to get the college education they hadn't had, to aim higher than the low income status they could never rise above, no matter how hard they worked. But lately..." In a heartbeat, she went from defensive to wistful. "My brother, Todd, is an accountant. My sister, Madeline, a teacher. But they also have families. I want a family, too."

A child, and a dependable man to love me, not one who chases storms...

"I guess that's what most folks want. Family, and a place to call home."

There's no place like home....

Rafe's words served to remind her of his loss.

And thoughts of home left her feeling hollow, her parents' home not hers anymore, her apartment not really hers, either, for she'd been too busy pursuing a career to add the touches that would make it so.

They sat quietly, and the setting sun enthralled her, gold rays shooting between clouds to cast a distant grain elevator in a violet silhouette. As the sky darkened, diamond stars winked between the clouds. "This is beautiful," she murmured.

"Yeah, it is." Rafe's husky tone drew her, holding more wonder than the horizon. He was looking at her.... "You spend much time chasing storms, you'll find yourself falling in love with the prairie."

She was falling in love with more than the prairie, Mariah thought, mesmerized. She was falling in love with the wrong kind of man....

Even as Rafe closed the distance across the small table that separated him and Mariah, he reminded himself of the careful way she'd brushed the dust from her silk shirt. He better understood the importance of her career after learning of her upbringing. But he could also see how her job had come to be on the line, that soft spot she had for children developing naturally into a need for a child of her own. Though she hadn't yet realized it, she'd already learned the real riches in life weren't material, but rather the people you shared life with. A lesson Ann had never learned.

But this camaraderie between him and Mariah was a dangerous thing....

He threaded his fingers into her thick, soft ponytail, feeling the warm back of her neck. Feeling her give in response to the slight pressure of his hand. She'd driven him crazy today, putting up her hair, silk clinging to her curves as she did. Despite the deal they'd made, he hadn't been able to forget their first kiss. The way she'd caught him off guard, like a sudden storm, like *magic*.... He shouldn't kiss her again.

But he tugged her closer, meeting her halfway across the table, covering her mouth with his. Caution jolted from his mind. Like cloud to ground lightning, the touch of their kiss was electric, negative to positive charges meeting, sparking, burning out.

Mariah pulled back, as hot and breathless as he, her eyes reflecting the desire and the wariness that clashed hot and cold within him. He knew what she was thinking. Outlaw storm chaser. Not a man she should get involved with if she wanted a family. And there was no way to prove differently, not when capturing tornadoes on film held such importance to Sunny.

Sunny.

Rafe breathed deeply. He couldn't afford to be wrong about Mariah's feelings for him, the way he'd been wrong about Ann's. Her job was important to her, saving it the driving force that had brought her here.

And in accord, Mariah said quickly, "I can't risk this."

She fought the urge to simply flee the emotions that threatened to sweep her away like one of Rafe's tornadoes. Sunny wanted this story. And Mariah needed it if she meant to keep her job.

"I have to focus on my work. You have to get your photographs."

And even before Rafe agreed, she read his thoughts clearly in his eyes, dark with determination to protect his daughter from her. She wasn't a risk worth taking for him, either.

Chapter Seven

"Why don't you clean off the windshield while I pay for the gas?"

Rafe tossed the words over his shoulder, striding toward the gas station to pay the attendant lounging inside.

With warm rain drizzling over the Oklahoma panhandle, dampening her black T-shirt and frizzing the neat bun of her hair, Mariah glared after Rafe's attractive backside as he pulled his wallet from the hip pocket of his khakis—the same ones he'd worn yesterday. Had sharing a motel room with him last night somehow qualified her as his hired hand?

She eyed the bug-splattered windshield. Then

she tossed the morning's collection of foam coffee cups in a trash barrel, dusted her hands on the back of her black jeans and climbed resolutely into the truck. Before they'd ever hit the road, he'd had her cleaning cameras and lenses and packing film, then storing it all in the truck with a fastidiousness that bordered on fanatical. He'd reattached a half dozen antennas to the truck, remounting the video camera and wind anemometer he'd all but tucked into bed with him last night. Next, he'd made a radio test, checked under the hood and tried out the wipers, headlights and emergency equipment. All this after he'd risen at the crack of dawn for a weather fix, connecting his laptop to the phone jack in the motel room. She hadn't needed bunk beds; he'd come in late and gotten up early, barely noticing she was there.

She only wished she could say the same for herself where he was concerned.

Rafe sauntered out of the gas station, two cellophane-wrapped sandwiches in one hand, the stale kind that came out of a vending machine, and two sodas in the other. Chase cuisine.

"Ham on rye or white?" he offered impatiently through the truck window. Unshaven, his hair disheveled, his clean white T-shirt already wrinkled, he looked as out of sorts as she felt.

"I'm not picky." She was hungry and tired.

Coffee hadn't qualified as breakfast, and having Rafe sprawled in the bed next to hers last night wasn't conducive to sleep.

He handed her a sandwich and soda, rounding the truck to climb in the driver's seat. He frowned at the bug-splattered windshield. "How am I supposed to videotape through that mess?"

"I don't do windows. And this truck needs more than the windshield washed." Mariah unwrapped her sandwich, Rafe's stare boring through her.

"You could help out, considering I let you come along."

"I *did* help out. But I'm not here to act as your personal slave." She eyed him shrewdly. "You're just trying to discourage me from coming along on the next chase."

"It so happens the remote camera can record valuable information if we get caught up in a storm—if the windshield is clean." Then he added all too casually, "It's a chaser's version of an aircraft's black box."

Mariah glanced uneasily at the forward-view camera, imagining them driving through the midst of a storm like the one they'd fled the other day, their fate recorded on videotape. "Now you're trying to *scare* me off."

"Why would I do that? I enjoy having someone

walk in front of the camera while I'm trying to
shoot, using all my hot water at the motel—''

"I did *not* use all the hot water."

"Constantly asking questions—"

"It's my *job* to ask questions—"

Rap. Rap.

The tap of knuckles against the driver's window
silenced them. A weathered face appeared, a
farmer pushing back his seed-corn cap as Rafe
rolled down the window.

"You and the Mrs. mind pulling away from the
pump to argue?"

"I am *not* his wife—"

"Sorry about that." Rafe dumped his sandwich
onto her lap, starting the truck and pulling forward.
Mariah made a hasty grab for the spill of waxy
cheese and limp lettuce, confining it to her once-
clean jeans as he pulled onto the highway.

The Mrs. Mariah reconstructed Rafe's sandwich,
thinking grumpily that she might as well be. Fixing
his food, cleaning his cameras. She'd even made
the motel beds this morning. *Mrs. Rafe Taylor.
Mariah Marie Taylor. Mrs. "Stormy" Taylor...*

That brought her to her senses.

Rafe seemed as eager as she to put the episode
behind them. They chased cloud formations all
through the Oklahoma panhandle, working west
again, slipping up into Colorado before heading

back into the Texas panhandle, never having con-
fronted a storm.

"We'll find a place to stop for the night," Rafe
announced as the day waned into a drizzly evening. "There's no sense in driving all the way back
to Amarillo with no change in the forecast in sight.
We'll probably head home tomorrow."

Back to Oz. Mariah brightened at the prospect,
while Rafe seemed disgruntled by the lack of pho-
tographable storms. There was a time she would
have thought he just missed the thrill; now she
thought about the tornado he'd witnessed as a boy,
of the telling way he seemed to have turned back
to his outlaw ways after the death of his beloved
wife. She understood that he wanted to gather data
to prevent more tragedy. It should have been that
simple. But the more she got to know him, the
more complex he seemed, the sense he held something back nagging at her, the risk-taking edge to
his personality coexisting with the side of him that
had created a "Land of Oz" for his grieving
daughter. The hook of her story seemed somehow
tangled therein.

The slowing of the truck drew her from her puz-
zling. She recognized the row of muddy, battered,
bug-splattered vehicles for the chaser convergence
they were, instead of the space oddities they ap-

peared with their antennas, cameras and wind anemometers.

Rafe pulled off the blacktop, and they got out, greeted by characters as quirky as their vehicles, all lamenting the lack of storms as the drizzling rain soaked unheeded into their clothes. Mariah felt something of an oddity herself, folks eyeing them from the few cars that passed by as if they were on exhibit—that rare, crazy breed of humans that chased tornadoes. Some, recognizing plates or emblems proclaiming them storm spotters, stopped to ask after the chances of a tornado, while others snapped photos through their car windows.

Rafe had introduced her as a journalist, raising some brows. But contemplation of her hadn't lasted long, too many tales of close calls and high-risk days gone bust to be shared. "Stormy's" popularity among his peers was undeniable. But it was when talk turned to the devastation of tornadoes recently ravaging the Florida coast that Rafe captured her admiration, touching her heart with his frustration and concern.

"With better data, warnings could be issued further in advance. Lives could be spared." Rafe pushed from where he leaned against the truck, and she could see his impatience with the repeated loss of lives, with the weather and himself. His expression darkened further with the arrival of a news crew van. "We need to get back on the road."

She'd clearly done little to sway his resentment of journalists.

They didn't drive far, stopping before dusk at the first small town with a motel posting a vacancy. The tidy place was a step above the Cactus in more ways than one—there were two rooms available.

After steaks at a small diner, Mariah retired to her room for a lengthy shower, slipping into the comfortable flowered pajamas she'd smuggled along. Taking a towel to her hair, she studied the room. While this was hardly a four star hotel, the room was tastefully decorated, with enough amenities to make a person feel pampered. She served herself a ginger ale and curled in a chair to relax.

But she quickly grew bored by the TV. And replaying the day in her mind only left her with that restless feeling of a story just out of grasp. She gazed about the quiet room. A very nice room. But just another lonely motel room all the same. Times like this, she could almost hear her biological clock ticking.

Her gaze drifted to the bed, then the telephone on the nightstand. Wistful longing squeezed at her heart. Rafe was probably talking to Sunny now....

Sighing, she raised the towel to her hair again, only to pause in her rubbing at the sudden beat of rain against the window. She lowered the towel by slow degrees. Lightning illuminated the square of window behind the dark drapes, accompanied by a drum roll of thunder. The elusive storms of the day had found them.

Clutching her towel, she rose and peered between the drapes to find rain sheeting across the blacktop, wind driving it beneath the protective awning outside. She let the drape fall. Surely Rafe would apprise her of any danger. There had been no watches or warnings on the TV—thus far.

She left a small lamp burning, turned the TV back on, and sat on the bed near the phone. All that talk over lack of suitable tornado warnings, still fresh in her mind, had her uneasy. Sharing a room with Rafe again wouldn't have been so bad after all. Perhaps she would ring his room, see what he had to say about this storm.

The door shuddered in its frame, startling her until she heard Rafe shout her name and realized he pounded on it from outside. Relief swept her, then she panicked at the thought he'd come to warn her of a tornado. She sprang from the bed, bounding to the door, flinging it open.

Heart thudding, she stared at Rafe, his shoulders hunched against the rain, his clean-shaven jaw brushing the collar of his fresh khaki shirt—an unbuttoned shirt that revealed his smooth tan chest.

The damp air enhanced the soap-scent of him, his slicked-down hair too wet for the short jaunt he'd made from the room next door. He must have showered.... Rain reached under the awning, pelting his clean jeans and shirt.

"Come with me." He'd raised his voice over the wind and rain she'd momentarily forgotten, her heart pounding for all the wrong reasons now.

"But—"

"It won't take a moment. Sunny's on the phone. She wants to say goodnight to you."

"Oh, of course." There was no tornado, after all. There was no reason for her heart to keep thundering in her chest. "I just need to…put on something warmer."

"Those clothes are all right—it's not cold, it's wet. Just put on some shoes." He reached past the door frame to snatch up the room key from a table. He grabbed her hand and she managed to shove her feet into her hiking boots before he tugged her across the threshold. They dashed beneath the overhang and by the time they crowded through the door to his room, Mariah was laughing, reminded of dashing through the rain as a child with Todd and Madeline to the safety of the front porch.

Rafe kicked off his boots and retrieved the phone from the bedside table. She took the receiver he offered, and her heart melted at the sleepy sweet sound of Sunny's goodnight.

Rafe tried not to stare, the way he'd felt Mariah staring at him when she'd answered her door. He'd pretended not to notice, but he could still feel the heat of her gaze on his chest and the cool rain against his back. That she'd run out into the storm to say goodnight to Sunny sent a warm gentle feeling through him.

In a grudging concession, he had to admit she was a good sport, despite the pitfalls of chasing she'd dealt with since her arrival. She wasn't even picky about food. He guessed you didn't grow up poor and be picky. Though she did seem to indulge in pretty clothes to make up for those hand-me-downs....

He noticed then that her pretty *clothes* were *pajamas.*

Soft-looking violet pajamas that did crazy things to her eyes and his pulse. Pajamas that revealed her shapely legs, feminine even with hiking boots on her feet. Pajamas that clung to her, dampened by the rain and her freshly washed hair.

Her hair. It was wild, beautiful, dampness turning it into a mass of glistening curls.

Wind rattled the windows and Mariah inched closer to him, clutching the phone, her voice faltering. Rafe silently groaned with the effort of keeping his hands off her. Maybe he shouldn't have scared her today with his talk of black boxes. He stopped at the first vacancy he'd seen tonight to avoid the torture of having to share a room with her again. Now here she was, close to him, smelling as sweet as she had last night. All night...

"Sweet dreams, Sunny." Mariah handed over the receiver. "She says we shouldn't talk on the telephone during a thunderstorm."

"She's right." Rafe pressed the phone to his ear, listening to his daughter, watching Mariah's nervous gaze skate to the window. "No, sweetheart, there isn't even a tornado watch, just the thunderstorm moving through."

Mariah smiled wanly, as if aware his placating words for Sunny were also meant to calm her. But she trembled along with the rumble of thunder.

"We should be home tomorrow. 'Night, sweetheart." Rafe replaced the phone, then faced Mariah. "Thanks. She wasn't going to give me any peace if I didn't let her talk to you."

"I didn't mind," she said wistfully, then she jolted with the next round of lightning and thunder. "I guess I'd better go back to my room."

Her words should have served as his cue to reassure her and walk her back to her room. But that warm feeling her kindness to Sunny elicited had burned into a welcoming glow. All he could think was that he wanted her to stay. Wanted her...

Lightning struck close by, its brilliance flashing between the cracks in the drapes. An explosive round of thunder followed. Anticipating, Rafe caught hold of her arm in the same moment the power failed. Darkness amplified her gasp, heightened the scent, the softness, the warmth of her to his senses. She flattened her hand to his chest, and each flicker of light revealed fresh emotions on her face. Apprehension, question, wonder, need...

"Cloud to ground lightning," he murmured reassuringly, recalling last night's kiss, feeling the charge build. "A negative spark is launched from a cloud...meets a rising positive spark..." Drawn by invisible forces, he leaned into her hand as he spoke, and met with no resistance. She was more intriguing, more dangerous than lightning. Yet he couldn't pull away. He pushed his hand into her thick, soft hair, grazing her mouth with his. "Their paths form a channel...superheating the air... creating shock waves..." And he was ready for the return stroke when it came, Mariah slipping her arm around his neck, kissing him back with a heat that stunned him.

And the thought burned through him—what if Mariah was different from the rest, the way Sunny believed? The way he wanted to believe...

Chapter Eight

It was good to be back in "Oz."

Mariah shut off her laptop. After lunch, she'd curled up in a white wicker porch chair, Sunny sprawled at her feet with a contented Oz. Now she lay back her head, closing her weary eyes.

She'd "interviewed" Wizard and Oz, and recorded her impressions of the past three days spent on the road, leaving out the lasting impression of Rafe's kisses. She needed more for her feature; the personal touches that gave a story heart. The kind that Rafe shied from, only raising *more* questions.

Mariah sighed, the afternoon hot, the breeze warm, the Kansas sky cloudless. A down day for Rafe...

The whirring click of a camera had her blinking
her eyes a fraction to peer hazily at Rafe. He stood
at the bottom of the porch steps, the sun spilling
over his shiny hair and broad shoulders as he
framed her and Sunny through the viewfinder of
his camera. She could imagine the strong rays
burning his back through his field shirt. He wore
pale denim shorts and his legs were brown and
sturdy above his boots, which were covered with
the same fine layer of dust that powdered all of
Kansas.

Including her. Self-conscious, Mariah sat up,
brushing at her sleeveless white shirt and blue
shorts. She couldn't do much about those freckles
on her nose, brought out by the sunny day. Or her
messy hair, strands tugged loose of her ponytail by
the incessant breeze. She could have worn better
shoes instead of the "ruby slippers" Dorothy had
given her. Amazing, how easily she'd fallen back
into her hand-me-down ways...

"Smile, Mariah." Sunny grinned, lifting Oz,
aiming his whiskery face at the camera. Rafe
snapped a few more pictures, but Mariah suspected
he'd gotten the shots he wanted before they'd realized what he was up to. She liked to compile
information for her features in the same fashion,
before self-consciousness set in and replies became
stilted or cheesy—like Sunny's cheeky pose, she

thought, grinning down at the picture the little girl made with her cat.

Another picture came to mind and she gazed into the camera lens and asked, "Is the tornado I photographed named after me? The way hurricanes have names?"

Sunny giggled. Rafe slowly lowered his camera. "Tornadoes aren't officially named, but they're often remembered for the towns they hit."

Or the lives they take, Mariah silently added, certain he was thinking of Ann. Deadly tornadoes had hit near Wichita before, but it was only now, when she actually knew someone who had suffered the loss of a loved one, that the reality of their destruction hit home. Hurrying to change the subject before Sunny's smile disappeared, she said, "I could use a tour of Tassel to add to my notes."

Rafe eyed her warily. "You've already seen all there is to see, driving in on 54."

"But Mariah hasn't been to the baseball diamond where I play little league. Or the gulch where we fish outside of town. Or the church where you and Mom got married." As her enthusiasm rose, so did Sunny, leaving Oz pouting on the porch floor. "Can I go tell Grandma we're going for a ride?"

Rafe seemed to struggle with his decision; he clearly didn't want to go sightseeing with her, revealing even more of his personal life. She imagined the idea of visiting the church where he married played into his reluctance, as well. But he gave in to his daughter's wishes, saying, ''Ask Grandma if we can use her pickup. The chase truck needs an oil change. Tell her we'll be back by suppertime.''

Sunny dashed off to do his bidding, leaving her to contend with Rafe as he grumbled, ''Satisfied?''

Peeved by his attitude, she frowned as he raised the camera and started snapping away again. ''Would you please put that thing away!''

''What's the matter? Does it make you uncomfortable to have your every move recorded? Analyzed? Exploited?''

''Yes!'' And it made her ashamed over every journalist that had made Rafe and his family feel like bugs on a slide. Still, she defended herself. ''But you're trying to make me feel that way. And you assume I'll do the same to you.''

Rafe raised his head, his gaze more intrusive than the camera. ''I just don't picture you saving your job by writing about Sunny's pets and the weather.''

I don't either. ''I distinctly remember you suggesting a piece of fluff like that would do fine.''

Rafe glared at her and she glared right back. But she knew her frustration with him had more to do with the way his mistrust came between them than with its effect on her work. She was grateful for the distraction when Sunny swung the screened door open, marching over, clutching a hairbrush and purple hairbands to match her T-shirt.

"Grandma said the keys are in the truck."

"Okay, sweetheart. I'll drive it over from the garage."

Rafe strode off as if nothing was amiss and, pleased, Sunny plopped down in front of Mariah's chair. "Grandma said I need my braids fixed."

Grandma said. Mariah caught her lip, wondering if Grandma had intended to tidy Sunny's hair herself. She took the brush Sunny handed her, and, when Grandma failed to join them outside, unbraided Sunny's thick hair, brushing the silky strands smooth before rebraiding them.

And for a few moments, that restless clock ticking inside her stilled. As she fastened the last purple band, she was aware Rafe had paused in cleaning the pickup's windshield—a fetish of tornado-chasing photographers—to watch intently. She hastily finished Sunny's braids.

"Thanks, Mariah." Beaming, Sunny trod down the porch steps, calling back, "I'll tell Dad to bring the fishing poles."

Mariah's answering smile faded when she noticed Sunny's grandmother watching through the screen, her brows raised. Dorothy gave the door a shove and stepped outside. "That child's taken quite a shine to you."

Considering you're a journalist, Mariah silently amended. And likely stepping on Dorothy's toes, taking over the motherly task of braiding Sunny's hair. Rafe clearly thought so.

Mariah stood, handing over the hairbrush. "Sunny seemed in a rush to leave. I wasn't trying to interfere. I realize she must look to you as her mother now."

Dorothy took the brush almost absently, taking in the sight of her son giving his daughter an impromptu driving lesson. After a moment she turned her attention to the brush, drawing Sunny's soft strands from the bristles. "You seem like a pretty smart girl."

But... Mariah held her breath waiting.

"But it's never been my intention to be a parent to that child. She lost her mother the night of the storm. She didn't need to lose her Grandma, too." Dorothy gave a practical smile to accompany her practical words. "I believe they're waiting for you."

"I—yes, they are." Mariah rushed down the steps. At the bottom she turned, smiling softly. "You should have been named after Auntie Em. Or maybe Glinda, the good witch."

Dorothy chuckled, tugging the hem of her plaid shirt. "Glinda's a mite frilly for me. I imagine there's a bit of Em in me, though. Run along now, before Rafe lets Sunny drive that truck down the highway."

If only Rafe imparted that same sense of approval, Mariah thought, hiding her frustration as she joined him and Sunny in the truck. For all her preconceptions of him, she kept seeing another side of him, the one that made careful, precise forecasts before a chase, who was protective of his child. Why couldn't he see her for who she was, the way Dorothy seemed to do, instead of lumping her with every other journalist he'd known?

Then he might feel as confused as she... Might be falling in love like she...

Sunny directed the tour, starting with the baseball diamond. Mariah could easily imagine herself cheering from the metal bleachers, the way Rafe and Ann must have. But they hadn't brought Sunny's ball and bat and glove, and watching dust blow across the diamond through the chain link fence didn't last long.

They drove to the service station to get minnows, heading west out of town to the gulch where they fished. Rafe steered the truck to the side of the road and they made their way down through a thicket of briars and cottonwoods. The trickle of water had been made deep enough by recent rain to drop in a line and try their luck. They sat in a row along the bank, the way Mariah knew Sunny must have once sat with Rafe and her mother. *Memories.* When Sunny tired of feeding the fish without luck of catching one, they moved on to the church.

The old-fashioned white church sat isolated on a flat grassy plot. Sunny rang the bell out front, then ran to pick sunflowers from along the white fence that bordered a small cemetery out back. Mariah knew the peaceful setting had little to do with the solemn mood that came over Sunny and Rafe, even before Sunny revealed, "My mother is buried here."

Mariah chose flowers carefully, adding to Sunny's bouquet, aware of Rafe's silent regard. She drew the bright blue band from her ponytail, freeing her hair, and helped Sunny twist it around the stems.

"This is pretty." Sunny admired their handiwork. "I'm going to get married here someday, like my mom and dad did." She glanced toward the cemetery, with its neat rows of white crosses and granite markers. "Sometimes I pretend my mom went to Oz in the storm, like Dorothy and Toto in the movie. But I know she's really in heaven, that she can't come back home." Sunny turned, beginning the trek to her mother's grave, Mariah knew.

Sunny turned back at the gate, serious as only Sunny could be. "I go to Sunday school here, too. Do you need to write this down, so you won't forget anything?"

"I don't need to take notes. I won't forget anything." Mariah spoke past the tightness in her throat. After a moment, Sunny pushed open the gate, a small child taking steps no child should have to take. She suddenly realized she'd become privy this afternoon to more than she wanted to know.

Discovering the hook of her story no longer appealed. She only wanted to do whatever it took to banish this child's pain, and Rafe's. For she was falling in love with Sunny as surely as she was falling in love with Rafe....

Mariah met his gaze, knew her every emotion burned in her eyes. But he only raised his face to the sky, as if looking for answers that a year of grieving hadn't resolved, his pain triggering an ache inside her.

"I'll always love your mother...."

Rafe hadn't spoken those words only to comfort his daughter. He was hiding his pain from the world, still in love with the wife he'd lost.

She should be grateful he was the wrong kind of man for her.

The slow-moving warm front brought more rain that night. A heavy, but harmless, rain, Rafe knew. But there was enough action in the sky to awaken Sunny and have her calling for him.

Pulling on gray sweats over his boxers, he emerged from his room to find his mother and Mariah stepping out into the hall. His gaze riveted a moment on Mariah, wearing her violet pajamas, her hair curling down her back. Her eyes darkened. He should have put on a shirt…. "Go back to sleep, I'll take care of Sunny."

Dorothy murmured reassuringly, then disappeared into her room. Mariah followed suit more slowly. Rafe stared after her a moment before hurrying down the hall.

He switched on Sunny's night-light and crossed the lavender carpet, hoping he appeared as big as he felt each time he entered this room with its miniature furniture and feminine ruffles. Big enough to scare Sunny's fears away.

He smoothed her hair, tucking her under her sheet with her stuffed Toto. "It's just the warm front moving on through, dropping some rain. By tomorrow, the sun will be shining again. It should be a little cooler than today. Cold fronts and warm fronts alternate.''

Nothing like a few meteorological facts to calm his daughter in a storm.

Sunny nestled back against her pillow, hugging Toto tightly. "I had fun today. I was sad sometimes, but mostly I had fun.''

"We had a nice break in the rain." But the day had left him exhausted, his daughter's pain and his own combining with the ache of wanting Mariah.

"Dad, I think you should check on Mariah. I think she's really afraid of storms. She sounded afraid when I talked to her on the phone the night it stormed on your motel.''

Checking on Mariah was the last thing he needed to do. He could picture her all too easily in the guest-room bed, lying back on the sheet, her dark hair raining over a pillow. "I wouldn't want to wake her.''

"She'll be awake. She might want to bunk in here with me tonight. She might sleep better then.''

That easily translated to mean Sunny would sleep better if Mariah slept in here with her. He was no match for the soft place Sunny touched in his heart. "You're probably right. I'll go ask her.''

"Dad? Will you chase down another tornado soon? Will you get another picture?''

"You bet I will." *Soon, he silently vowed.* He'd

do anything to lessen the fear in Sunny's eyes and the pain in her heart. And he'd do anything to keep her from being hurt again.

Leaving the small light burning, he went down the hall. A faint glow shone beneath Mariah's door. He dragged his hand across his whiskered cheek. Knocking on the door seemed at odds with the direction his thoughts had taken. Still, he rapped lightly, knowing this was what Sunny needed—for now. "Mariah? It's Rafe."

Mariah opened the door almost immediately, pulling a matching wrapper over her pajamas. For a moment, he felt lost in a sea of violet flowers and blue eyes.

"Sunny thought you might be scared of the storm."

"Smart girl." Mariah sounded nervous, stirring his protective instincts the same as his daughter had. "No tornadoes?"

"No tornadoes. Only the last of the warm front pushing on," he assured her, the way he had Sunny. "She thought you might want to bunk with her—more to the point, she got scared and wants you in the room with her."

"Of course I'll bunk with her. I'll just turn out the light."

They reached for the wall switch in the same moment, his hand covering hers as they were en-

veloped in darkness. Soft, warm, sweet smelling...
Mariah. The catch of her breath was no less potent
than her nearness. He wanted to take her hand,
press it to his bare chest. Instead he drew back,
and managed to rasp out the words, "Follow me."

Sunny was sitting up in bed again, waiting for
Mariah. "My Dorothy doll is on the bottom bunk.
You can sleep with it."

"I'll be careful not to squash her," Mariah said,
nose-to-nose now with Sunny as she stood beside
Rafe at the bunk bed. "Thank you for letting me
share your room again."

"You're welcome."

Rafe absorbed the sight of Mariah brushing back
Sunny's hair, soft emotion on her face for his child.
He'd seen the yearning in her eyes today, the con-
cern for Sunny and for him. She cared about them.
She was falling in love with them....

But what if he was wrong? He'd believed in
Ann's love for him, too. Today had brought back
memories, and his daughter's pain had been almost
more than he could bear.

"Tuck in Mariah, too," Sunny murmured, lying
sleepily back against her pillow.

A timely flash of lightning added to the glow of
the night-light, illuminating each curve and hollow
of Mariah's face. There was tenderness for his
daughter and apprehension of the storm. And when

she turned to him, there was desire, the same need that consumed him of late.

Rafe made himself step away with a husky, "Good night."

"Good night," she whispered loudly, so that Sunny could hear, he was sure. Then she slipped into the bunk, pulling the sheet to her shoulders, curling to face the wall.

Rafe left the room, closing the door. He sank against the wall, lightning flickering and thunder rumbling outside the hall window. He was more determined than ever to gather the photographs that helped his daughter cope with her fear of storms, and her grief. But he was beginning to fear that it was Mariah who posed the greatest threat to her well-being.

Chapter Nine

Rafe wiped sweat from his brow with the sleeve of his white T-shirt. Giving the hood of the chase truck one last buff with a cotton cloth, he stepped back to survey his handiwork, fresh wax layered over the vehicle's battle scars. Mariah had been right, the truck needed more than the bug-splattered windshield washed.

He'd meant to burn off a little frustration over Mariah, to get her off his mind. But now that the task was done, his attention wandered with a will of its own to find her, to see if she noticed his hard work.

Her laugh drifted from inside the barn. She stood helping his mother and Sunny weave braids into the pony's mane. Wizard switched his tail, otherwise unmoving, almost as if he enjoyed the fuss. Amazing, the things males withstood for women. However meticulous he was about his camera, weather equipment and the windshield, he hadn't washed the chase truck since...whenever the last rain fell.

More laughter had him frowning. Everyone seemed to be enjoying yet another down day but him, right down to the pony. Everyone seemed to be *bonding* but him, his mother's approval of Mariah growing, Sunny's adoration of her the greatest worry in his life. He was falling under Mariah's spell, too, wanting to believe the emotion he read in her eyes, wanting to let her into his life—and Sunny's. And that was the crux of his frustration; only he knew the kind of devastation that could result if he misjudged Mariah's feelings for him, the way he had Ann's.

The wind gusted, carrying the strong scent of wax, stirring miniature dust devils. Instinctively, he studied the sky. And sensed something brewing. To the distant south, gray clouds layered the horizon.

Rafe met Mariah's gaze over a whirl of dust and heat. Her eyes full of question, she gave the pony a pat, murmuring to Dorothy and Sunny, and started over.

Her hair was alive with the wind, the dark strands blowing like curled streamers from the black band that held her ponytail. Her ivory tank and olive shorts molded against her. He knew the moment she spied the thick clouds, saw her eyeing the birds that had gathered on the phone line. She wrinkled her nose when the smell of wax reached her over the pungent scent of grass. From behind her, Sunny's laugh rang hollowly on the thickening air, and Mariah smiled as she closed the distance. He wondered if she realized how attuned she'd become to the effects of the weather. And he realized how attuned *he'd* become to *her*.

"There are storms coming, aren't there?" she asked without hesitation.

"I don't think they'll push this far north. But there'll be some action all across Oklahoma."

Mariah pushed back her windblown hair, gathering it with her hand, squinting as she concentrated on the far-off clouds. "How can you tell?"

"Cloud sequences," he murmured, but his gaze was no longer on the storm to the south. "Altostratus preceding cumulus and cumulonimbus... The drop in barometric pressure... Your hair."

"What?" Mariah slowly let go of her hair, freeing the glorious strands to the hand of the wind.

Rafe curled his fingers into the cloth he held. Then, unable to resist, he raised his other hand, capturing a softly coiled strand. "Your hair. It goes crazy when the humidity rises."

"I know." Her voice came on a wisp of breath, quick and uneven. "I can never do a thing with it."

"You don't have to," he assured her huskily. The wind snatched the curl free. Sunny's laughter carried to him, reminding him of her needs. "I'd better go check with the NWS. Map out a plan."

"I'll be ready to leave when you are."

He'd kind of figured that, Rafe thought as she walked toward the barn. She wasn't easily discouraged, a trait that had obviously stood her well in building her career, and would help her now to save her job.

Leaving the worrisome scene of his daughter running to meet Mariah, he went to the house and got down to the business at hand—finding a storm to chase. And with any luck, a tornado to photograph for his daughter.

Mariah was good as her word, ready and waiting to go when he headed for the truck half an hour later. She'd traded her ruby slippers for her more practical boots, and carried a denim shirt for a jacket to pull over her tank. He'd traded his white T-shirt for a brown field shirt with handy pockets to wear with his jeans. His adrenaline was already pumping. A call to Jeremy had confirmed an outbreak of storms, he informed Mariah. He'd head south, try to position them to the best advantage behind a storm cell, converging with Jeremy somewhere along the way.

He gave Sunny one last hug. With her pain from yesterday's outing still fresh in his mind, he promised to try his best to "capture" another tornado for her. Then he and Mariah boarded the truck and he gunned down the drive.

Mariah settled back in the seat. There was something unnerving about deliberately driving into a storm, apprehension already a knot in her stomach. As they dipped into Oklahoma, Rafe pointed out vertically developing cumulus clouds, or towers, that were predecessors to thunderstorms. He networked a patchwork of roads, some paved, some not, in his effort to follow a particularly impressive tower as it built, only to collapse without producing a storm. His disgust evident, Rafe pulled off the highway for gas west of Enid.

"Damn." He shoved his hand through his hair, giving it that spiked look born of frustration. He got out of the truck and jammed the nozzle into the gas tank, bracing his hand against the roof, his head lowered as he silently fumed.

Mariah climbed from the truck, her boots hitting pavement, the heat smacking her in the face. More than the hot weather had Rafe's patience frayed today. She hadn't missed the way he'd held Sunny close before leaving. Her sightseeing tour of yesterday had stirred memories of Ann, and she knew it was those memories that drove him now. Guilt plagued her; if she could have conjured up a storm for him, she would have.

Walking around to his side of the truck, she lifted her heavy ponytail from her neck, catching a hot gust of breeze. She faltered, Rafe's burning gaze adding to the heat. She let her hair fall. "I'm going to get a cola. Do you want anything?"

The way his eyes darkened, she knew she should rephrase the question. Instead she waited, her breath backed up in her lungs, her pulse pounding. After an eternity, he replied gruffly, "I could use a cold drink, thanks."

He turned away to replace the nozzle. With a quick rush of breath, Mariah headed for the cool confines of the gas station. Other vehicles were pulled up to the pumps, folks watching the sky warily as they filled their tanks. Mariah gazed at the puffy white clouds to the east, the same type that had already fooled them. According to reports on the radio, Rafe's prediction of a severe weather outbreak had materialized, but they had yet to happen onto a successfully developing storm.

Mariah filled cups with ice and cola and went to stand in line at the counter, manned by a lone cashier. A radio tuned to a country station had her mentally humming along as she waited. Rafe pushed through the door and strode to her side, bypassing an impatient woman behind her. Mariah braced herself for a complaint over his cutting in line, only to watch wryly as he flashed a charming smile that had the woman suddenly happy to wait.

Then he turned to her, frowning. "What's holding things up?"

She frowned back at him. "I would think that was obvious."

Rafe raised his brows, but before he could offer her a comeback, the radio interrupted with a National Weather Service warning—a tornado reported on the ground east of Enid.

Mariah locked gazes with Rafe, a spontaneous connection that broke when he strode to the head of the line, dug a bill from his pocket and slapped it on the counter. "That should cover it."

He hustled her out the door, to the accompaniment of a few grumbles—though Mariah doubted any came from the woman he'd charmed or the clerk he'd left a fifty-dollar bill. She juggled the drinks in her hand, struggling into the truck and slamming the door. She found holders for the drinks and fastened her seat belt as Rafe drove back onto the road.

"We'll try and get close to the updraft base—

that's where a tornado's most likely to drop.'' Rafe gripped the wheel, scanning the sky, and Mariah sensed a desperation in his search that left her feeling hollow. *Ann...*

They caught up with the storm outside of town, the puffed clouds piling high into a menacing ivory mass she recognized from her first chase with Rafe. The fear that gripped her was familiar, too, her throat closing on a gasp, rendering her speechless. A condition Rafe would no doubt appreciate.

But it didn't last long. Mariah peered through the windshield. ''The clouds seem *twisted.* Does that mean the storm is rotating?''

''Rotating,'' Rafe finished in unison. Suddenly, he slowed the truck and steered off the road. Ahead, other vehicles had pulled off, too, people emerging to stare at the sky.

''There!'' Rafe caught her arm, pointing as a funnel dropped from the dark cloud base. He reached for his still camera. She missed the warm, strong grip of his hand as the tornado hovered eerily over a field, then swiftly retreated back into the cloud.

''Damn.'' In the process of leaning out the window, Rafe lowered the camera and sat back in the seat. His dark expression said plainly that he'd missed the shot.

''Is it over?'' Somehow, she doubted it was.

"This is only the beginning," Rafe confirmed her thoughts grimly, sending a chill up her spine. He slung the strap of the camera around his neck, ready for next time. She wondered how close to the storm this mood he was in would take them.

They spun off the roadside, spraying gravel and white dust, creating a minivortex of their own.

"We'll try and stay parallel to the storm," Rafe explained. "But the way it's tracking, we need a northbound road to catch up to it."

Mariah riffled through the maps on the dash, grabbing Oklahoma, unfurling it on her lap. She traced the road with her finger, muttering, "Here's Enid...we must be about...here. Just ahead! There should be a road to the left."

No sooner did she speak than a narrow sign appeared, designating a northbound road.

"Hang on." Rafe made the turn, the truck fishtailing on gravel. They straightened out of the skid. The blare of a horn had Mariah twisting in the seat, Rafe peering in the rearview mirror.

"Jeremy," they announced in unison.

Rafe grabbed the mike as Jeremy transmitted, "Don't get too close, Stormy. You don't want to be in the path if we get a touchdown."

"Roger that." Rafe stepped on the gas, and she realized the cloud mass was picking up speed as it churned. Rafe angled the video mounted on the dash, hoping for another funnel to drop, she knew. The weatherman kept a running advisory on the radio, warning folks to take shelter, even as Rafe accelerated on a course of interception with the storm.

Green fields gave way to trees, the road plunging into a wooded area. Atop the next rise, the storm loomed darkly, shrouded by the swaying trees. *Leaning trees.*

"The wind's picking up," Mariah murmured.

Rafe scanned the treetops. "It's feeding into a funnel—the trees are bending in the direction of a tornado, somewhere over that hill."

A tornado. Just over the hill. A tornado she knew he meant to photograph. A chill snaked down her spine as wind hit the truck. This was crazy. *He* was crazy. Hadn't she known all along?

He glanced at her, as if he'd been so absorbed in the storm, he only just remembered she was there. He slowed the truck, steering to the bumpy side of the road. Dust billowed, then was whipped away by the wind. He stopped and shoved open the door, leaving the truck running. "Come on."

Warily, Mariah followed. Jeremy had pulled over behind them. Now he swung out of his pickup, a gleam in his eyes, his black hair blowing. "Do you see those trees? We're headed toward a funnel. We need to get parallel to the storm again. But the next turnoff is miles away.''

His voice echoed Rafe's frustration. Mariah realized they were as close to the storm as they could safely be.

Rafe caught hold of her arm. Wind flattened his field shirt to his chest, furrowed through his hair. Seconds passed in which she committed the grim line of his mouth, the determined set of his shadowed jaw, the intensity of his gaze to memory. For a moment, she thought he might kiss her. Then he pushed her into Jeremy's arms. "Keep Mariah here. I'm not going to miss this shot.''

No! Rafe wasn't behaving rationally, his focus on Ann, instead of the daughter who needed him. Even as her heart seemed to crack, she strove to make him see reason. "Rafe, stop! Think of Sunny—''

He was already running for the truck.

"Rafe, wait!'' Jeremy added his protest, holding her back in her effort to follow and halt Rafe's driven chase.

"You've got to stop him,'' Mariah pleaded. Rafe leaped into the truck, slamming the door.

"I could easier stop the tornado,'' Jeremy muttered. "Rafe hasn't done anything this foolish since before Sunny was born. Rafe!''

"Let me go!'' Mariah demanded. When Jeremy

held fast to her arm, she told him, "You'd follow if it was Trixie."

His grip loosened a fraction, her words apparently hitting home. Mariah took advantage and jerked free, running. "Rafe, wait!"

She raced after Rafe to no avail, the tires of the chase truck spinning, dust rolling as he shot onto the road. Jeremy caught up with her and she halted, battered by grit and frustration. "He'll be killed!"

They stood frozen, unable to do more than watch as Rafe gunned the truck up the steep dirt road toward the swirling black clouds at the top.

Then it started to rain, not drops but debris. Branches, brush, broken fence boards, dirt—their hidden tornado tossed it all up and away from the vortex and overtop of the hill. Jeremy dragged her farther back out of range. Mariah cupped her hands over her mouth, stifling a cry, envisioning a tree limb smashing through the chase truck's windshield.

"Stop, damn you!" Jeremy yelled—at the storm or at Rafe, she couldn't tell.

As if in answer, the brake lights flashed, the truck skidding, sliding sideways, narrowly missing a tree limb before Rafe got it stopped. He backed down the hill, out of reach as the last of the debris rained down. *Safe…*

The wind slowed, the trees bending gently now,

the storm twirling away. The truck came to a stop. Rafe pushed open the door. He stepped out, curling his hand overtop the door to watch the departing storm. Jeremy slipped his hand from her arm and murmured, "He's okay."

Mariah lowered her hands from her mouth. She started toward the truck, each step taking on purpose with her growing sense of anger over the way he'd risked his life with no regard for his daughter, his loved ones, his friends. *For her...*

By the time she reached the truck she was fuming—and feeling alive in every pore, every cell. She pushed back frizzing strands of her hair. With her heart still pounding and ten years of her life likely lost to worry and fright, she strode up to Rafe and grabbed his arm. He faced her, but it seemed as if she dragged him from a dazed state, some far-off place she couldn't go.

Ann.

"Why would you do such a thing? Take such a risk for a picture?" She braced herself for the answer, certain he would say he did it for Ann, out of loss, out of love, unable to let go of the past. Maybe hearing the words would stop this fall she was taking into love with the wrong kind of man.

Rafe let go of the door. A weariness came into his eyes, and his voice grew hoarse as he told her, "I do it for Sunny."

She let her hand slip from his arm as he turned away, walking partway up the hill to stand staring skyward. Suddenly it was all clear. The way Sunny seemed to believe her dad was invincible. The intent way she asked if he'd gotten a picture of a tornado; not out of fear for him, but because it somehow banished *her* fears, lessened her grief, each time he "captured" a tornado on film.

Rafe was being a hero for his little girl....

And Mariah knew then there was no stopping her fall.

Chapter Ten

"A rotating supercell..." Rafe muttered as he
drove, eyeing the expanding white cloud mass to
the north. In the two days since they'd left Jeremy
chasing storms on into north central Kansas, he and
Mariah had crossed Oklahoma and the Texas panhandle, working north into Colorado, encountering
only a few showers around Amarillo along the
way. But as they traveled the backroads south of
Dodge City, Kansas, close to home, the supercell
built at an alarming rate, taking on a life of its own.

Concern for Mariah's safety, and that of his
mother and Sunny, had him pressing his boot to
the accelerator, leaving a plume of gravel dust
hanging in the air. He'd contacted his mother on

the radio; she and Sunny knew a tornado watch
had been issued, knew Rafe and Mariah would be
home soon. His only regret in foregoing a chase
was that he'd failed again to "capture" a tornado
for his daughter.

Mariah, folding a map upon the lap of her black
jeans, glanced at the afternoon sky with obvious
apprehension. But then, she had a right to be worried after the way he'd blindly chased that funnel
the other day. Hoping to ease her mind, he told
her, "I'll try and get us home before this weather
breaks loose."

She contemplated the dense white clouds and
dark wall cloud with more knowledge than she had
a week ago, likely recognizing there was little
chance they would outrun the storm. "Is a tornado
probable?"

No sense in trying to sugarcoat the danger. Taking the same tack he would take with Sunny, he
offered the technical explanation he knew she
would prefer to empty reassurance. "The Saturn-
like rings halfway up the cloud mass indicate ro-
tation. The collapse of the domelike cloud overtop
of the tower could signal formation of a tornado."

Her gaze locked with his for a second, fraught
with awareness.

The radio, tuned low to a Dodge City station,
added its own ominous warning.

"The National Weather Service in Dodge City, Kansas, has issued a thunderstorm warning effective until 5 p.m. The storm, spotted south of Dodge City and moving east, has been associated with heavy rain, hail and high winds that may produce tornadoes. The tornado watch continues until 7 p.m."

Even as the warning was issued, wind gusted, rocking the truck.

Rafe battled to keep the truck on course, then pressed his foot on the accelerator. He kept tabs on the storm out the window, increasingly aware he ran a losing race.

"Is something wrong with the engine?" Replacing the map on the dash, Mariah stilled, staring through the windshield.

"Damn." Steam curled from beneath the hood, to be quickly snatched by the wind. The thermostat shot to red. Rafe steered to the side of the road, bouncing to a stop on the bumpy grass shoulder.

"What is it? What's wrong?"

He switched off the ignition. "The engine overheated. Must have blown a hole in the radiator hose." He hoped it was nothing more. "I'll have to fix it before we drive on. The engine will seize up if I don't."

Pushing a roll of duct tape into the pocket of his khaki pants and grabbing a rag from under the seat,

Rafe opened the truck door. Wind molded his black T-shirt to his chest. There wasn't much time. "Bring me that gallon jug of water from in back—but stay clear while I uncap the radiator."

He had the hot cap twisted off and balanced on the fender of the truck when Mariah joined him, jug in hand. The wind whipped her ponytail into a frenzy that told him more than any scientific data could have. Aware time was of the essence, Rafe wiped the hose dry, tossing the soaked rag aside. "We'll let things cool a minute. Then I'll tape the hose and top off the radiator." *And we'll get the hell out of here.*

Impatient, he retrieved his still camera from the truck, photographing the storm as it closed in. If it kept on its easterly track, they might miss the worst of it. But supercells were notorious for their erratic change in course—a fact Mariah had learned first-hand the day she'd arrived. Now he'd put her in danger again. He lowered the camera in frustration, muttering, "I just checked under the hood this morning."

"This isn't your fault. You keep the truck well maintained—even if you don't wash it often enough," Mariah told him, adding with a grumble, "How are we supposed to get any pictures through this mess?"

He turned to her. She sounded like *him.* She'd

gotten another rag and was cleaning the windshield. In that way a storm had of heightening sen-
sory perception, his awareness of her seemed to
increase tenfold. Each shiny curl of her hair, the
pearlescent sheen of perspiration lying over the
tiny gold freckles on her nose, the way her lips
parted as she worked. Her black T-shirt was as
wrinkled as his. The crimson polish on her nails
had vanished along with her naiveté of the storms.
He'd only fooled himself, thinking he could keep
her from becoming too much a part of his life, and
Sunny's. She already was.

"I won't take any chances like I did the other
day, chasing that funnel," he said huskily.

Mariah slowed her circles with the cloth, raising
her face to the wind to look at him. "I know you
won't. I understand that you did that for Sunny."

And he suspected she was doing this as much
for Sunny as she was to save her job. Seeing the
hero worship in her eyes, and more, he warned her,
"I'm no hero."

Yes, you are. Mariah gazed after him as he faced
the storm, shutting her out. He was probably thinking of Ann, she thought painfully. Instinctively,
she sensed the story of her life at hand with this
heroic, storm-chasing man and the adorable, but
grieving, daughter for whom he'd created a healing
"Land of Oz." She ought to be ferreting out the

answers to the missing link that would give her heartwarming feature the kind of edge needed to save her job. But her sense of objectivity seemed to have blown away with the wind. All she wanted to do was help Rafe and Sunny find happiness again.

And at the moment, help came in the form of a clean windshield. Mariah went back to her polishing.

But the wind suddenly cooled and strengthened, and she abandoned her task. The wall cloud had started to churn, a dark, dangerous merry-go-round. The storm was moving their way....

"A right-mover." Mariah sang out the words in unison with Rafe.

She threw her rag in the back of the truck. Rafe tossed his camera on the front seat. He dug the tape from his pocket, locating the damaged area. Mariah held the hose in place as he wound tape around it.

The wind dragged her clothes against her body. As Rafe poured water into the radiator, she shook her blowing hair from her face to check out the storm.

"There's no funnel," she told him, relieved. "Just that huge wedge-shaped cloud a good half a mile away."

Looking up, Rafe grimly banished her optimism. "That *is* the funnel."

Oh, my. Mariah stood frozen, entranced by the wedge-shaped menace bearing down.

Rafe finished recapping the radiator and slammed down the hood. The plastic jug he'd set aside tumbled away in the wind. He grabbed her hand. "Come on!"

It was all the encouragement she needed.

They fought the wind to round the truck and open the door, a hard gust blowing it shut behind them. The truck shuddered. The crazed wind seemed to spin the world off balance.

Rafe cranked the key in the ignition. The radio blasted to life with a high-pitched emergency alert.

"The National Weather Service in Dodge City, Kansas, has issued a tornado warning for Ford County. The National Weather Service radar in Dodge City detected a tornado twelve miles southeast of the city. Take shelter immediately if you are in the path of this storm."

Static filled the air. Mariah switched off the radio. Rafe wheeled back onto the highway, a two-by-four cartwheeling alongside as they tore down the road. Then it disappeared.

"There must be a road where we can turn off." Mariah reached for her trusty map.

"There are only tractor paths for miles—we

could wind up stranded in mud.'' Rafe gripped the wheel. He'd failed to protect Ann. He wasn't going to let anything happen to Mariah. ''There's an abandoned farm just ahead where we can take cover.''

''I'll get your camera.'' Mariah thrust the map aside, reaching for his still camera.

''Forget it!'' The lane appeared, sandwiched between crooked fence posts. ''Hang on!''

He slowed enough to make the turn, driving over shrubs and sidewalk to cross the lawn, braking near the storm cellar. He tugged Mariah out of the truck, then flattened her against it, a branch whizzing by. The air was alive with debris. Missiles...

Mariah's face, close to his, was wide-eyed with fear. Curving his arm around her, he turned her toward the cellar, only to watch the rotted door shred, carried off by the wind.

''Rafe!'' Mariah grabbed his shirt, pointing, the wedge bearing down, ripping up field and fence, spewing it skyward.

''The house! Run!'' He half-carried her, stumbling up broken steps, dodging missing porch boards. He booted open the door and they tumbled inside. The remaining glass in the windows shattered around them, wooden lathe ripping from walls crumbled bare of rotted drywall. More missiles... Sheltering Mariah's body with his, he propelled her down the hall, turning the knob on the first door he came to.

Yes. The basement...

"Watch for missing steps!" he warned above the roar of the storm, navigating the way downstairs. At the bottom, he pulled Mariah to the northwest corner, near a rusted water heater where they crouched on the musty concrete among dust and cobwebs. Her gaze met his. Fear, amazement... The whirl of her emotions transcended the storm. He pressed his lips firmly to hers, then he held her tightly, his back between her and the twister.

Dust rained down, the house splintering and cracking above them. An invisible hand tugged at his clothes, at him. *Mariah*...

Then it suddenly released them.

Rafe slumped against Mariah. The sounds of the storm decreased to a quiet as ominous as the tornado's roar. He could feel the warmth of the sun on his back, the warmth of Mariah beneath him. *Alive*...

She moaned and he eased his weight off her. Gently, urgently, he turned her in his arms. She blinked hazily up at him, her eyes full of concern.

"We're okay," he told her, gently brushing dust from her cheek.

"You didn't get a picture for Sunny."

He felt something poking against his chest then—his camera. Somehow she'd held on to it, through the blowing debris, through her fear, through a *twister*. His heart turned in his chest. She'd held on for Sunny.

Sunny. He saw his worry mirrored in Mariah's eyes—the need to know if Sunny and his mother were in the path of the storm. "Let's get out of here."

He helped Mariah to her feet. They squinted into the sun that now streamed between rafters and shone through a rocket-shaped hole in the floor overhead. Surveying the rubble around them, they locked gazes in disbelief. The stairs were gone; the rusted water heater vanished.

Rafe set to work, steadily stacking fallen lumber and concrete blocks into a makeshift stair. Taking hold of Mariah's hand, he started to climb, pulling her along behind him.

Near the top, he released her, levering himself onto the main floor. There was rubble everywhere. The skeleton of walls seemed intact, the floor sturdy enough, aside from the gaping hole. Grateful Mariah wore boots instead of her ruby slippers, he cautioned her, "Watch out for glass and nails."

Then he hauled her up beside him. They got to their feet. Rafe left her a moment, making his way to the back of the hall to gaze out the shell of a

ROBIN NICHOLAS   165

window. The tornado had plowed a wide brown path across gold-topped wheat fields—a path that veered northeast. He let out a breath, silently giving thanks. "The storm's moving away from Tassel."

"Sunny and Dorothy will be safe."

Mariah's relieved reply drifted from a room at the front of the house. Rafe turned in exasperation, catching a glimpse of her through the sketchy walls as she held his camera aloft to snap pictures of the damage. "Your curiosity must have made you a trial to raise," he muttered.

He was ready to get them out of the untrustworthy remains of this house and on their way home. Then he heard the sound of an engine, growing closer, someone driving down the lane. Through the frame of the front door, he spied a familiar blue pickup sliding to a halt. "Mom?"

"Rafe, it's Dorothy and Sunny!" Mariah confirmed.

Indeed, there was Sunny, opening the truck door, climbing out in her bibs and white T-shirt. Dorothy called after her to wait, but she ran toward the house, her braids bouncing.

"Daddy, are you hurt?"

Hurt? He'd started forward. Now his world ground to a halt with Sunny's anxious cry.

The rafters overhead groaned. Swayed.

"Sunny, stop!" He plowed forward, flinging aside rafters, tromping down debris.

"Sunny, stay back!" Even as she called out to his daughter, Mariah scaled fallen lumber, trying to get to the door before Sunny. Wood cracked ominously from above. Sunny's footsteps thundered across the porch.

"Sunny! Mariah!"

They seemed a million miles out of reach as a rafter plummeted with horrific slow-motion quality.

Sunny crossed the threshold.

Mariah lunged for her.

His daughter tumbled out the door, out of danger.

The rafter struck Mariah, crumpling her to the floor.

So much blood.

"Why won't she wake up?" Sunny cried, inconsolable.

"She's okay. She's okay." *Dear God, she's unconscious.* Nothing seemed to be broken. Rafe knelt on the porch, lifting Mariah gently against his chest, trying to placate his daughter. Trying not to panic.

"Here." Dorothy had returned from her pickup. In that magical way of mothers, she handed him a clean handkerchief. "Sunny, come here to Grandma."

While his mother folded his sobbing daughter close, Rafe pressed the cloth to the cut on Mariah's forehead. "Did you get the hospital on the radio?"

"We'll meet them on the way in." Dorothy gave his shoulder a hard squeeze. "Head wounds always bleed a lot. She'll be fine."

He realized she said it for Sunny, and erased the fear from his face. He told himself it could be worse. She could be broken, bleeding inside. He gazed down at her pale face. *God, what if she was?*

"Come along now, Rafe. Let's get her to the hospital."

"Hurry, Daddy."

Blood seeped through the handkerchief at an alarming rate. Sunny needed him, yet he couldn't move, couldn't breathe, his whole being focused on Mariah. *Open your eyes.*

Sunny cupped her small hand over Mariah's, something so right and so wrong in the gesture, it pained him.

Mariah had knowingly risked her life to save his daughter; her feelings for Sunny had known no bounds. Sunny's young heart didn't know bounds existed. And his heart seemed to have forgotten, for there was no limit to the love he was feeling for Mariah now.

Mariah.

She moaned softly.

"Mariah." Rafe tightened his arms around her.

"Sunny, look, she's opened her eyes," Dorothy said.

"Daddy, she's awake."

He gazed into Mariah's eyes. *Pain. She was hurting.* He eased the pressure on her wound, but it only bled more. "You'll be fine." He pressed down again, looked back into her eyes. *Love without bounds. For him.* He wanted to believe what he saw.

"Let's get you to the hospital."

It was later, at the hospital in Dodge City, when he came to his senses.

Sunny, finally allowed by Mariah's bed in the emergency room, all but crawled upon it, standing by the lowered siderail, leaning her elbows on the narrow mattress.

"Are you *really* all right?"

"Yes, really."

"Are you going to write about getting stitches in the magazine, too?"

"I think I'll stick to writing about you and Wizard and Oz." Mariah's laugh, though tired, was encouraging. Yet Rafe felt a sinking in his heart.

Nothing had changed. Mariah was still trying to

save the job that had changed her lifestyle, still wanted a dependable man to give her the baby she longed for.

The truth was, love had bounds. And those bounds were uncertain. For Sunny's sake, he couldn't afford to misjudge them.

Chapter Eleven

They kept waking her up.

Mariah pushed away the hand someone rested against her cheek, feeling fretful as any child who hadn't had enough sleep. "Go away."

"But I have to look at your eyes."

Sunny. Dear, sweet Sunny. If anything had happened to her... But it hadn't. She struggled to open her eyes, remembering, the way she remembered each time they woke her, that she had pushed Sunny out of harm's way. Rafe had called out to Sunny, his voice full of fear, full of love. Then he'd called out her name and she'd heard concern for her, too.

She remembered the pain. She remembered seeing love for her in Rafe's eyes....

"Dad! Mariah won't open her eyes." Sunny ran off, her footsteps fading.

She'd scared Sunny. She had to wake up, despite her aching head and the fatigue weighing her down. Stitches, she recalled. Ten of them, on her forehead, done beneath glaring lights in the emergency room at the hospital in Dodge City. Dorothy had driven them there. Rafe had held her in his arms. Sunny had held her hand.

Mariah gingerly touched her bandaged forehead. *Ouch.*

She was awake now.

She levered herself up from the pillows mounded on Dorothy's cozy couch. She still wore her black jeans and T-shirt, dusty from the old house, bloody from her wound. She shouldn't be on the couch.

"Hold on there."

Mariah sank back into the cushions as Rafe and Sunny crossed the room. Sunny bent to peer at her, so close her hazel eyes almost crossed. Mariah smiled as her pint-size nurse decided, "They aren't...what's that word?"

"Dilating." Rafe bent to peer at her, too. "Feeling better? Headache? Dizziness? Any nausea?"

"I'm *fine.*" She felt better, seeing the worry leave Sunny's face. She just needed a bath. And some sleep. Rafe eyed her shrewdly and she admitted, "Maybe a little headache."

Rafe turned to Sunny. "Tell Grandma I'm taking Mariah upstairs now. You can bring the aspirin when it's time."

Sunny ran from the room.

"Maybe you shouldn't have been so stubborn about not staying in the hospital."

"I don't recall being stubborn." Mostly, she recalled being glad Rafe stayed by her side.

"You kept saying you wanted to go home."

Home. She'd wanted to come back *here,* with *them.*

Rafe reached out, sliding his finger beneath the wayward curls curving along her cheek, tucking back the wavy strands. "I'm glad they didn't have to cut your hair."

Her mind, already hazy, went blank. She managed to say, "I'm sorry to be so much trouble."

"Another inch and—" His voice went hoarse and her heart momentarily stilled. "You were lucky. And we were glad you got to come home. If we'd left you at the hospital, Sunny would have wanted to stay, too."

Rafe suddenly bent and swept her off the couch, holding her firmly against him, his arms warm around her shoulders and beneath her legs. She leaned heavily against him, his husky voice flowing over her as he said, "Thank you. You may have saved Sunny's life today."

"You're welcome. Thank you for saving me from the storm."

His heart beat steadily against her hand as he carried her up the stairs. She couldn't keep her eyes open, she was so tired. Yet her every sense seemed magnified, the way she'd noticed it heighten before a storm. The musty scent of the basement clung to her and Rafe's clothes. His breath was warm and comforting upon her hair. She could only sigh as he sat her on the bed, lifting her shirt over her head, slipping another one on.

Rain. Rafe's green T-shirt.

He lay her back on the bed. Tugged her jeans down. Her socks off. Then he whispered, "Be right back."

Moments later, a warm cloth was smoothed over her face. The antiseptic smell from the hospital disappeared. So soothing, so careful. Down her neck, so warm. Next her arms... Mariah gave herself over to Rafe's gentle hands, opening her eyes to watch him in the soft lamp light. His hair was mussed, streaked by dust and sun, his face covered with stubble and smudged with dirt, his eyes weary and dark with worry. He needed care, too. Needed her to return the love she could feel in his touch...

She placed her hand against his cheek, her

thumb to the corner of his mouth. His beautiful mouth. He covered her hand with his, and there it was again—love for her shining in his eyes.

Then he lowered her hand, the light in his eyes extinguished before he turned down the lamp. "Get some sleep."

And he left her alone.

Mariah blinked back tears. She'd seen his love for her, heard it, felt it. Yet he held his love back.

Despite everything, he still didn't trust her, still couldn't let go of his feelings for Ann.

All that love she'd seen and heard and felt meant nothing at all.

Mariah scooped her hair into a neat bun, inspecting her wound in the mirror the next morning. Her hairdo only seemed to emphasize the bruise and stitches near her temple.

With a sigh, she pulled on a navy shirt with her khaki shorts. She'd been careful not to get the wound wet when she showered. Now she applied a clean bandage and turned to her next chore—fold the clothes she'd washed in Dorothy's machine, then pack them. It was time to load up the rental car and head back to Wichita. She'd been right all along; there was nothing here for her in "Oz."

She had things neatly piled on the bed when

Sunny burst into the room, a blur of purple in her favorite T-shirt. "Grandma said to ask if you are hungry."

Sunny halted, then walked to the bed, staring hard at the stacks of clothes. "What are you doing?"

Mariah's heart clenched. She didn't want to go. More importantly, she didn't want to hurt Sunny by leaving. "I need to go back to Wichita now, write that feature about your dad, you and Wizard and Oz."

"You can write it here." Tears glistened in Sunny's eyes. "You can use Dad's computer. You don't have to *leave*."

"That's sweet of you, Sunny, but I really have to go back—" *Home?* Mariah focused her burning gaze out the window, to the colors of Rafe's over-the-rainbow farm. "Back to my apartment in Wichita."

"But I don't want you to go!"

Mariah staggered as Sunny flung her arms around her, holding on as if the child thought she might disappear. She held Sunny close. *And I don't want to leave.* Her voice trembling, Mariah promised, "I'll come back and visit."

Though she didn't know how she could bear to return to Rafe and Sunny, only to leave them again.

"No, you won't!" Sunny sobbed against her. "You'll be like my mom!"

Like Ann? Did Sunny fear she might die?

Sunny's arms tightened as she cried. "Mommy wasn't *ever* coming back to Tassel. I heard her say it when she talked on the phone."

Mariah stilled, shocked, the meaning of Sunny's painful words sinking in. The night Ann drove off in the storm, she had been leaving Sunny and Rafe....

Rafe. He stood in the doorway, solid and sturdy, clad in denim. A hero. Not the kind of man a woman would leave. But the vulnerable look on his face and the exquisite pain in his eyes confirmed the truth. Ann had left him the night she died out in the storm.

The missing link. The edge that would sell her story. Now she understood.

Rafe crossed the room, gently prying Sunny loose. She clung to him and he held his little girl with a protectiveness that forever touched Mariah's heart.

The story of her career.

It's hard to tell how low a person will go when they're trying to save their job.

Rafe's words haunted her, and for a bleak, dark moment, Mariah saw herself losing everything— her job, Rafe and Sunny.

But loving Rafe was uncertain. If he only had the heart to see how much *she* loved him, and Sunny.

And in that moment she realized there was no choice to make.

Chapter Twelve

That afternoon, Rafe braked the truck to a halt
beneath the cottonwood by the garage. He lifted
the envelope he'd picked up from the post office.
What if Mariah's tornado picture hadn't turned
out? He couldn't remember any exposure settings;
with Mariah to distract him that day, he'd pretty
much shot by instinct. With luck, he'd checked
them subconsciously before giving her his camera.
For Sunny's sake, he hoped so.

His daughter had been distraught this morning,
revealing what she'd known all along. That her
mother had been leaving her—them—when she
died.

It still stunned him to realize that Sunny knew

the secret he'd harbored this past year about Ann. Even his mother hadn't realized Ann had been leaving him, and Sunny. His daughter had been carrying a burden he'd often found too heavy to bear.

And now Mariah knew, too.

She had the story that would save her job. And her return to Wichita would be yet another heartbreaking burden for Sunny's small shoulders. Another heartbreak for him...

Rafe drew a deep breath and opened the envelope. He slid the pictures onto his lap.

Mariah's Wizard of Oz tornado.

There were photos of Mariah, too. The ones he'd taken when he should have been shooting the approaching storm. His photographer's eye had been drawn to her. The storm all around her, the wind blowing her hair, her blue eyes wide and innocent, with that glint of determination that had told him she intended to stay. *He'd* been drawn to her, right from the start.

He still was. And the longer he stared at her picture, all he saw was a woman who'd been determined to save his daughter's life, who'd risked her life to do so.

What a fool he'd been.

Mariah would never do anything to hurt

Sunny—not even to save her job. She loved his daughter too much to hurt Sunny.

Did he dare to believe the love he'd seen in her eyes for him? He had to talk to her—

"Dad!" Sunny came running from the house. Rafe pushed open the truck door, only to stand rooted. Mariah's rental car wasn't parked beside the garage. She was gone.

Pain consumed him. This was what he'd been afraid of; that Mariah would leave him the way Ann had. He needed Mariah, loved her.

And Sunny did, too. She jogged up to his side, her eyes still shadowed from the morning's tears. She gazed at the picture he handed her and some of the light came back into her eyes as she said, "Mariah's picture looks just like *The Wizard of Oz* tornado."

"Yes, it does." Sunny's love for Mariah radiated from his little girl. He needed to make sure she didn't view Mariah's departure in the same light as her mother's. "Mariah didn't mean to hurt us by leaving, you know."

"You mean the way Mommy did?"

"Ah, Sunny." Rafe gathered his daughter close. "Mommy didn't mean to hurt you either. She just needed something we couldn't give her."

"Mariah needs us. She's not afraid of storms when she's with us. And she helped you take pictures and drive out of the hail and kept me safe when the beam fell. You keep each other safe when you chase storms."

Daddy, are you hurt? Rafe groaned. At least Sunny understood now that he wasn't invincible. If he'd only had the brains to realize his daughter didn't need him taking foolish risks in his work to banish her fear and pain. She needed him to go on with his life—especially now that she wanted Mariah to be a part of theirs.

"Mariah needs other things, too," he explained carefully. "She'd like to get married someday and have a baby. It takes a lot of love for two people to get married and bring a child into the world."

Sunny glowed. "*We* love Mariah, right, Daddy? She could marry *you,* then she could have a baby and *me,* too. She was sad when she left. I think we should take her this picture, Dad. Then we should bring her back home."

With Sunny's blessing he finally had the courage to let go of the past, to tell Mariah he loved her. He knew he wouldn't have to be afraid Mariah would leave him and Sunny. For there was a difference between her and Ann. Ann hadn't loved him enough. He knew in his heart that Mariah did.

"I think maybe you're right."

* * *

Mariah put on her ruby slippers with her jeans and white T-shirt and went outside to curl up in a chair on the porch of the Victorian house where she rented the downstairs. The afternoon showers had stopped, the sun peeking through, casting a rainbow in the sky.

Somehow, it made her want to cry.

She needed to do more than just sit on the porch. A week had passed since she'd left "Oz." Her wound was healing nicely. She'd turned in her feature and her editor had loved the heartwarming tale. Rafe's painful secret, the "missing link" that would have given her story an edge, had been absent, and her editor hadn't commented on the lack of scandal. But then, Plain View wasn't a tabloid. Hadn't she known that all along?

She wondered what Rafe would think of the copy she'd sent him—

No, she needed to get on with her life. Add some homey touches to her apartment. Find that dependable man to love, have a baby…

Sighing, she lay back her head and let the sounds of the afternoon waft over her. The birds she'd seen perched in a flock on the branch of a cottonwood warbled like singers in a chorus line. Cars rolled by, some stopping, some not. Laughter echoed, children playing in a yard nearby.

Longing washed over her then. Here she was, with the proverbial rainbow right overhead, and all she wanted was to be back in "Oz." Because she didn't just want a baby. She wanted to have Rafe's child. She wanted to be a mother to Sunny. She wanted Rafe....

Mariah squeezed her eyes tighter to hold back the tears. Resolutely, she brushed back her frizzing hair from her face with her fingers. It was going to rain.

Funny, but she could almost smell it.

"Dad, she moved. She isn't sleeping."

Sunny.

"Why don't we go see?"

Rafe.

She didn't want to open her eyes, afraid she'd wind up like Dorothy in *The Wizard of Oz* and discover she was only dreaming.

Footsteps thundered with heartwrenching familiarity up the steps and across the porch floor, stopping before her.

"Mariah, it's me, Sunny. And Dad."

Mariah opened her eyes. Rafe, wearing a khaki shirt with his jeans, carrying an envelope. Sunny was wearing her gingham bibs and a white T-shirt, her hair in "Dorothy" braids. "I thought you were in 'Oz'."

Sunny giggled. "We were in Tassel. Now we're here. Grandma said to say she misses you. Can I go jump rope with those girls next door while you talk to Dad?''

Mariah straightened in her seat. This was definitely not a dream.

''Why don't you go ahead and jump rope,'' Rafe suggested to Sunny. ''Just stay where you can see me.''

Sunny dashed off. Mariah considered Rafe's boots, then the envelope in his hand. ''Are you headed to Trixie's, to meet up with Jeremy and chase storms?''

Rafe chuckled. ''Jeremy's been taking a lot of down days lately.''

To spend with Trixie and Jess, she thought wistfully.

She eyed the envelope. He probably had photographs to give her. But he could have mailed those.

She had to know. ''What brings you here, Rafe?''

He grinned. ''I just followed the Yellow Brick Road.'' Then more seriously, he added, ''I came to explain about Ann.''

She didn't want to talk about Ann.

He could see the uncertainty in Mariah's eyes. But he could see the longing, too. Still, it was the ''ruby slippers'' on her feet that gave him the courage to explain. ''I'd loved Ann since we were kids.

Thought I had it all when she finally agreed to marry me. But for her, our marriage was all about getting out of Tassel. I didn't see that until it was too late.''

"Her leaving and the accident—that wasn't your fault.''

"Maybe in time I'll accept that I couldn't have prevented the accident. As for Ann leaving me, I've been afraid to put Sunny through that again. Afraid to chance it myself. Until now.''

Rafe handed over the envelope. She needed to know that he trusted her. "I thought you might want your picture of the tornado for your feature.''

Mariah slipped the photo out. *"The Wizard of Oz tornado.''*

"I gave a copy to Sunny.''

"And I sent you a copy of the feature. It won't go to press without your approval.''

"I don't need to read it beforehand. I know you would never write anything that would hurt Sunny or me.''

"You're a hero, Rafe. For the sake of science and for your little girl. That's what I wrote in the feature.''

"I'm no hero.'' But his chest swelled with her words anyway. "I took a lot of foolish risks lately, thinking it would help Sunny. But I think what she really needs is *you.* I know I do.''

He pulled her out of the chair and into his arms. "There's no place like home for me, Mariah. But if you're willing to share my life, I'll do everything I can to support your career." His voice took a husky turn as he told her, "And Sunny's willing to share her hand-me-downs if you still want a baby."

Just click those ruby slippers and you'll be home.

Mariah let the pictures slip to the chair. She knew he'd be careful in his work, the way he'd been careful after Sunny was born. She trusted him, knew he trusted her. She wrapped her arms around him and kissed him, returning a love that knew no bounds.

"There's no place like home for me, either."

* * * * *

Don't miss the reprisal of Silhouette Romance's popular miniseries

When King Michael of Edenbourg goes missing,

Royally Wed
The Stanbury Crown

his devoted family and loyal subjects make it their mission to bring him home safely!

Their search begins March 2001 and continues through June 2001.

On sale March 2001: **THE EXPECTANT PRINCESS**
by bestselling author **Stella Bagwell** (SR #1504)

On sale April 2001: **THE BLACKSHEEP PRINCE'S BRIDE**
by rising star **Martha Shields** (SR #1510)

On sale May 2001: **CODE NAME: PRINCE**
by popular author **Valerie Parv** (SR #1516)

On sale June 2001: **AN OFFICER AND A PRINCESS**
by award-winning author **Carla Cassidy** (SR #1522)

Available at your favorite retail outlet.

Silhouette®
Where love comes alive™

Visit Silhouette at www.eHarlequin.com   SRRW3

100th BOOK

Join Silhouette Books as award-winning, bestselling author

Marie Ferrarella

celebrates her 100th Silhouette title!

Don't miss
ROUGH AROUND THE EDGES
Silhouette Romance #1505
March 2001

To remain in the United States, Shawn O'Rourke needed a wife. Kitt Dawson needed a home for herself and the baby daughter Shawn had helped her deliver. A marriage of convenience seemed the perfect solution—until they discovered that the real thing was *much* more appealing than playacting....

Available at your favorite retail outlet.

Silhouette®
Where love comes alive™

Visit Silhouette at www.eHarlequin.com   SRRAE

Silhouette
bestselling authors

KASEY
MICHAELS

RUTH
LANGAN

CAROLYN
ZANE

*welcome you to a world
of family, privilege and power
with three brand-new love
stories about America's
most beloved dynasty,
the Coltons*

*Brides
of
Privilege*

Available May 2001

Silhouette®
Where love comes alive™

Visit Silhouette at www.eHarlequin.com
PSCOLT

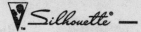

where love comes alive—online...

shop eHarlequin

- ♥ Find all the new Silhouette releases at everyday great discounts.

- ♥ Try before you buy! Read an excerpt from the latest Silhouette novels.

- ♥ Write an online review and share your thoughts with others.

reading room

- ♥ Read our Internet exclusive daily and weekly online serials, or vote in our interactive novel.

- ♥ Talk to other readers about your favorite novels in our Reading Groups.

- ♥ Take our Choose-a-Book quiz to find the series that matches you!

authors' alcove

- ♥ Find out interesting tidbits and details about your favorite authors' lives, interests and writing habits.

- ♥ Ever dreamed of being an author? Enter our Writing Round Robin. The Winning Chapter will be published online! Or review our writing guidelines for submitting your novel.

SINTB1

Silhouette invites you to come back to Whitehorn, Montana...

MONTANA MAVERICKS

WED IN WHITEHORN—
12 BRAND-NEW stories that capture living
and loving beneath the Big Sky where legends
live on and love lasts forever!

MM

And the adventure continues...

February 2001—
Jennifer Mikels *Rich, Rugged...Ruthless* (#9)

March 2001—
Cheryl St.John *The Magnificent Seven* (#10)

April 2001—
Laurie Paige *Outlaw Marriage* (#11)

May 2001—
Linda Turner *Nighthawk's Child* (#12)

Available at your favorite retail outlet.

Silhouette®
™ *Where love comes alive*™

Visit Silhouette at www.eHarlequin.com   PSMMGEN3

R_x PRESCRIPTION ROMANCE

Get swept away by
these warmhearted romances featuring
dedicated doctors and nurses....

LOVE IS JUST
A HEARTBEAT AWAY!

Available in April 2001 at your favorite retail outlet:

HOLDING THE BABY
by Laura MacDonald

TENDER LIAISON
by Joanna Neil

A FAMILIAR FEELING
by Margaret Barker

HEAVEN SENT
by Carol Wood

Visit us at www.eHarlequin.com

RCPRE2